Wicked Distractions

WICKED WAYS

ANGELA ADDAMS

Wicked Ways
ISBN # 978-1-83943-950-6
©Copyright Angela Addams 2021
Cover Art by Louisa Maggio ©Copyright February 2021
Interior text design by Claire Siemaszkiewicz
Totally Bound Publishing

WICKED WAYS

Dedication

This book is dedicated to Diana K.

Chapter One

Five years before

The second Adam locked eyes with the mysterious woman dressed up as a dark angel, he knew he was about to get fucked...in all the right ways.

Sure, he was wearing a lame-ass pirate costume that was at least two sizes too small for his bulky frame, and yeah, he wasn't supposed to be at the Halloween party to begin with, but this woman was staring at him like she wanted to eat him alive. Adam just knew that she'd come for him. He didn't know how he knew. It could have been the way her eyes drilled right into him, smoldering and full of lust, and completely locked on his. Or maybe it was her skimpy little costume, all tight-looking black leather, holding on to her curves in a way that made his dick weep — and totally the kind of getup that would drive him wild. Then again, perhaps it was simply the pulse of his aching cock, acting as some kind of lightning rod for a horny female in his sights that had him so sure. This woman was a totally dangerous kind of hot, and she was all his.

The room was completely packed with people, but Adam's dick was at full attention, straining against the flimsy fabric of his costume, so ready to sink into her. He'd thought the party was going to be lame. *Man, was I wrong.*

When he started to get up from his seat, she shot him a look that let him know he needed to stay put. She was coming to him.

Oh yeah, baby.

The party was pumping. The music was loud, the bass thumping hard and drinks were flowing. Adam was feeling really fucking good watching this woman come toward him. The crowd moved around her as she approached. Her hips swayed and the wings jutting from her back moved with her, making it seem like she was actually flying toward him. Everything she was wearing was black, from her halo to her sexy-as-hell stilettos — everything except for her pouty lips, which were painted a deep cherry red. Adam licked his lips. He bet she'd taste like cherries too. She had a halter-top vest on that had a zipper down the front. One zip down and her tits would spill right out. Fuck, he wished she'd move faster. He wanted her on his dick, and he had no problem with fucking her right there in the corner of the room. No one would notice, and if they did, they definitely wouldn't care.

She lifted her hands, running them along her hips and up her sides. Her tits weren't huge, but she had enough cleavage to make his mouth drool, thinking about licking all that soft, flawless skin. She moved to the side to avoid another girl who was dancing, and it gave Adam a nice view of her rear. Her ass was just visible under that skirt of hers, like one tug up and she'd be exposed. He was praying she wasn't wearing panties. *Fuuuuck, please let her be bare.*

She was sex. Pure sex. And even though she was wearing a mask over her eyes, Adam somehow just knew he'd never met her before. She wasn't from Grimshield. *No way.* He knew all the girls around town. Even though he'd been gone for ten years, he knew he'd never met this one before he'd left Montana. Besides, this party was a high-school reunion of sorts, and he was sure he hadn't gone to school with *her*. He would have remembered a girl like that.

He had to wonder, though, just where she'd come from.

The room was packed. There were so many bodies moving to the music and she was only a few feet away. He was sitting on a sofa chair, like a king, just watching over everyone, waiting for the gorgeous creature to make another move.

And when she got close enough, she stopped, but just for a second—long enough to give him a once-over that confirmed everything he already believed. She was going to ride his dick right there, right now. He was the luckiest guy alive.

She climbed onto his lap. No hesitation... She just hiked her skirt, flashed her lacy pink panties and climbed on up. Adam's dick was weeping for real. Her pussy was so hot that he could feel it radiating against his pants. She was wet.

She didn't speak. She just leaned in and kissed him, the fiercest kiss he'd had in a while. Her tongue was in his mouth, stroking him, and all he could think about was how good it felt...and how great her lips would be around his cock. All that cherry-red lipstick surrounding his dick? *Yeah, super fucking hot.*

She broke the kiss and looked down at him, her dark eyes full of lust and determination. She held up a condom that she'd pulled from fuck-knew-where and had her other hand playing with the zipper on her vest.

This was a sure thing. A quick fuck. His heart was hammering so hard, his dick was pulsing and he was desperate for the heat of her pussy. He grunted something meant to be affirmative, not trusting his voice to come out right.

She unzipped her vest. Her tits were glorious, a handful of flawless porcelain. Her nipples were ripe little berries. Adam was all hands and lips, sucking on her sweet buds, playing with her until she was rubbing herself against him. And when he slipped one hand between her legs, fuck, she was so damn wet, soaking her panties so much that he could have wept with joy.

It was so fucking hot—her little moans and purrs in his ear, the way she bit her bottom lip and how her hips moved when he yanked the panties aside and slipped his fingers into her tight, wet hole. It was a fucking fantasy come alive. This night could not get any more perfect.

Until it did.

She tugged at the flimsy drawstring of his costume and his dick came out like it was spring-loaded. It was hard and slick with pre-cum, and he was dying for her to suck him off. But her lips didn't come close. Her hands were all over his cock, rubbing him so good that he could have spewed just from that. But she shifted herself back, ripped the condom package with her teeth then slipped it onto his aching cock so fast that he barely had time to think about it. He pulled his fingers out of her and sucked down the taste of her. Their eyes were locked. She was totally in it with him. She tasted like heaven and he wanted more.

Her eyes were drilling him as she lifted her hips and rammed herself hard onto his dick, right down his shaft until he was completely sheathed to the hilt. The sexiest fucking smile curled her lips and she slowly drew her body back, rubbing his cock until she was almost off him before sliding to the hilt again. Yes, she was totally going to fuck his brains out.

This…this was a night for the record books.

There they were, surrounded by other people, and this amazingly gorgeous creature was riding him like her life depended on it. Her sweet little pussy was so damn tight that it was like a leather glove squeezing his dick each time she rolled her hips. And her tits? They were right at his mouth, so he had to suck them in. His hands were on her ass, moving her harder, faster. Then she leaned in closer, so close that her lips were at his ear and she moaned a long, sexy sound. Her pussy was doing a spasmy thing of the most intense ripples and he realized that she was coming so fucking hard. So he let loose too, just let his climax go and filled the fucking condom.

He had his hands on her hips and he pulled her down to kiss those sweet lips again, but she pushed back, her hands on his chest to stop him.

"Nah-uh, big boy," she purred.

He looked up at her, his mind fuzzy, feeling euphoric, wanting to know who this sexy woman was and where they could go for round two.

"What's your name, baby?

She just got a smile on her lips and pushed herself up and off him before adjusting her skirt. She did up her vest next, concealing her glorious tits from his view.

He moved forward, doing his best to stop her from leaving him, his dick still hard, wanting more.

"Come on, honey. Tell me who you are." No way this girl was leaving without giving him her digits.

She laughed, leaned in close and said, "Why don't you just call me Ugly Duckling, Adam?"

Adam froze. The smile slid from his lips. Clarity came like a slap to the face. There was only one girl he'd ever said something so vile to. "Missy?"

The curl to her lips turned into a sneer, all the answer he needed. Then she spun on those impossibly high heels and walked away.

He watched the crowd swallow her.

He'd just been fucked all right, by the one girl who hated his guts. The last time he'd seen Missy Alderton, she had not looked like a sex goddess. When he'd seen her, she'd been a scrawny teenager and a pain in his ass. Now at almost ten years later, Missy had definitely grown up, and she was sure as shit *not* an ugly duckling.

Chapter Two

Present day

Adam glanced at his phone as he walked through the lobby of Cowan Enterprises. He had a shit-ton of things to get done, starting with a meeting he'd been putting off with one of the new security camera manufacturers who'd been courting his boss, Sabine, for months. They wanted a deal and Adam was just about ready to start negotiating with them.

He frowned. Three missed calls from his mother. *Strange.*

He and his mom remained close, despite the physical distance between them. She was the only person in his family who didn't give him any grief about his chosen profession or his connection to Sabine. She was a strong lady, someone Adam admired greatly, and she didn't call three times in a row *ever*.

Adam hit her number then raised his phone to his ear. "Mom, what's going on?"

"Oh, honey, things are going sideways here." She paused. Cleared her throat. "You think you could come home?"

Home. Grimshield, Montana, a place he'd been avoiding, for many damn good reasons, for a very long time.

Adam stopped walking, his stomach lurching. Things had to be bad for his mom to ask him that. "What happened?" His thoughts immediately went to his father, who had been having heart issues for years now.

"It's your brother. He's...well, he's gotten into some trouble."

"What kind of trouble?" Adam growled, feeling a mix of annoyance and indifference. His brother Tommy was always looking for a money scheme, some way for him to cash in big for very little effort. He'd gotten into trouble more times than Adam could count, but this was the first time in a long time that their mom had called Adam to bail him out by coming home.

"He's gotten mixed up in something." Her voice was strained. "He won't tell me what's going on exactly, but there's this group of men sniffing around here, and your father says they're here because of Tom. They say he owes them a lot of money and that if he doesn't pay up, they're going to do something to him."

"Call the sheriff." His indifference shifted somewhat. Adam had known that eventually Tommy would stir up enough shit to get his parents involved. Honestly, he was surprised it hadn't happened already, what with Tommy's gambling issues and risk-taking on different sure-thing ventures. There'd been situations that had required Adam to step in, sending money to his mom so she could bail Tommy out of a jam here and there, but nothing that had escalated like this.

"We have called the sheriff. These guys—thugs, really—they've settled in town and they're causing problems everywhere."

Of course his brother had gotten caught up in some kind of shit like this. If he didn't know any better, Adam would say it was his brother who had brought the guys into town himself.

"Adam, they said they'll take the ranch to get what's owed. Your dad... He's...well, you know him... He's thinking he's a big, tough guy still, but his heart can't take this shit." She paused. "I'm sorry for cussing, but I haven't slept. I'm just so scared." Her voice was trembling.

His mom admitting fear was maybe the most terrifying thing Adam had ever heard in his life. As much as he didn't want to clean up his brother's mess again, he wouldn't let his shit impact the family. Not like this. "Where's Tommy now?"

"I don't know. He wasn't here when the guys came to talk to your dad and he's not here now."

Adam sighed. *Fuck my brother and his bullshit.* As much as Adam wanted to just throw some money at the problem and continue on with his life, he knew he wasn't going to feel good about that at all. "Mom, don't worry. I'll be there tonight. I'll take care of this." Because that was what Adam did. He took care of problems.

"I've already made up your bed."

Adam let out a snort.

"In the loft, of course. I know you won't stay in the house."

"Actually, Mom, I think it'll be best if I get a room at Lacey's for now."

15

"Lacey's! That's where those men are staying. They're giving her a hard time too."

Lacey was a seventy-year-old tough-as-hell badass. If she couldn't keep the trouble-making men in line, then they had to be pretty bad. "All the better reason for me to stay there then." He cleared his throat. "Besides, I don't think Dad will want me staying at the ranch. You remember what happened last time."

"I don't give a damn what your—" She halted her next words, took a few deep breaths then said, "Sorry, son. You're right. Best you stay at Lacey's until we figure some things out. Your bed is made up here, though, just so you know."

"Thanks, Mom. I love you too. I'll see you tonight."

The meeting with the security manufacturer would have to wait. He ended the call with his mom and immediately called his boss. "Hey, Sabine, I've got a situation."

* * * *

As expected, Sabine had told him to take the company jet. He was en route to Grimshield within the hour. And that left him with about four hours of thinking time.

His brother was a continual fuck-up, always getting himself into some kind of trouble from the time they had been kids. For some reason, that only made their father prouder of him. It never made any sense to Adam, but when Tommy fucked up, their dad not only came to the rescue but also gave Tommy a pat on the back when it was over. Sure, there would be some kind of lecture about how things had been done back in his day, but in the end, Adam would always find Tommy and their dad sitting around drinking beer, shooting the shit and laughing about all the other fucking idiots in the world. Adam was sure they considered him one of those idiots too.

It didn't matter what Adam did, how much he achieved or how he'd gotten his life sorted out and on track. He was never good enough in his father's eyes. Sure, he hadn't always been the most responsible person, and he had made some terrible choices when he'd been younger, but he'd worked hard to overcome all that. Favoritism didn't begin to describe the relationship between his dad and Tommy. In fact, their father seemed to blame Adam for most of the things that Tommy did wrong, even if Adam wasn't in the same state at the time.

Needless to say, it put a strain on the brotherly love between Adam and Tommy as well.

But that wasn't the only reason Adam wasn't too keyed up to be heading home. Another huge problem with returning to Grimshield was, predictably, all about a woman.

Missy Alderton. Or, he should probably say, *Sheriff* Missy Alderton — the woman of his fantasies. The woman of his nightmares.

He hadn't been back home for five years. He hadn't seen Missy since that night at the Halloween party where she'd fucked his brains out. He'd wanted to see her, oh fuck, had he wanted to. He'd tried calling her after the party, even paid a visit to her place before he'd left town, but she'd made it clear that she wanted nothing to do with him. And she wasn't interested in any kind of apology for the shitty things he'd said when they had both been younger.

She'd gotten her revenge. *Wham, bam*...and that had been it. She'd told him to leave town and forget about her. He'd left town, but no way would he forget that night. It was seared into his memory and taunted him in his dreams. He wanted more from Missy, but he knew she wouldn't give it to him.

Wanting something he just couldn't have… Well, that sucked. Big time.

Despite how much he still wanted her, he wasn't too keen on invading Missy's space now. It was too bad his brother was such a fuck-up, because inevitably his brother's troubles no doubt impacted her world as the only law enforcement in town. There was nothing he could do about that, though. He could only hope that maybe in the five years that had passed, she'd gotten over it or at least cooled off enough for them to be on speaking terms.

What he'd said to Missy all those years ago had been awful, sure, but by now she should be open enough to listen to his apology. That was what he was hoping for, anyway. He knew the reality was that Missy held grudges and always had. Since he'd known her from the time she had been a kid, he felt pretty confident that that was a quality she likely wouldn't have grown out of—not toward him, anyway. Besides, it wasn't like he was hard to get hold of. All she'd have had to do was make one call to Cowan Enterprises and she would have gotten through to him…if she'd really wanted to.

But she hadn't tried, not once since that night.

By the time the plane landed and Adam had gotten his rented SUV, he was feeling a heightened mix of anxiety and frustration. There was too much on his mind but too little for him to do about it until he knew exactly what was going on.

He'd called ahead to make sure Lacey had a room, so that was his first stop. He wanted to stash his things and get a bit of information from Lacey before he ventured out to the ranch. She'd know what the gossip around town was and who these thugs were that Tommy was all tied up with. Adam would gather a bit of intel and maybe have a bite to eat. There was no way he wanted to arrive back at the ranch just in time for dinner. The last time he'd had dinner with his dad, threats had been made, insults flung and the table had been flipped, none of it done by Adam.

He wasn't particularly stoked about being back for more abuse from his dad. So yeah, he was stalling.

Fuck... So many reasons not to come home.

He pulled his rented SUV into Lacey's small parking lot down the side of her hotel. There were three other vehicles there — two SUVs, similar to Adam's but black, and a cherry-red sports car that was very shiny, very expensive-looking and very much out of place.

He grabbed his large duffel bag out of the back and made his way to the entrance of the hotel. Lacey's hadn't changed in the time he'd been gone, not that he'd expected it to. It was the only building left that still looked like it belonged in an old western movie. With a walk-out porch fronting it and a big ole' sign that read 'Lacey's Saloon', one might actually think that they'd stepped back in time. It had been in her family for generations, and while she'd updated the interior to keep up with the times, the outside had that old-world charm that travelers found irresistible. The hotel above the pub had five rooms, and they were usually always booked.

Adam knew Lacey always tried to keep a room free for local needs, but all the same, he was lucky that she'd had a room available for him to rent for the few days he planned on staying in Grimshield.

He paused with one foot on the first step and took in the main street. Nothing had changed, really. The pharmacy was still bustling, and so was the fruit market. There was an old theater that only showed two movies at a time and somehow managed to stay in business, despite all the streaming services available. The people seemed younger somehow. There were more families mingling about than Adam remembered—lots of little kids running around with their moms mostly. At some point, folks must have decided that Grimshield was a safe place to raise kids, because Adam never remembered the main street being quite so busy.

He shook his head. It had never once occurred to him to stick around, even without all the shit from his dad and the baggage with Missy. He'd never really felt like he belonged anyway.

As Adam neared the doors of the pub, he could hear raised voices inside, loud enough to draw his complete attention. Through the glass he could see a guy slowly being surrounded by four others. Something was definitely going down. The body language was all aggression, and Adam could see that the one guy didn't stand a chance against the men surrounding him.

Adam's bodyguard instincts kicked in. He let his duffel drop to the porch before he opened the door and stepped inside. "Hey, fellas, don't you think the odds are a little unfair here?"

At the sound of his voice, the man being targeted turned his head slightly and Adam caught his profile.

Because of course it is.

"Stay out of this, Adam," Tommy growled. "I've got these assholes right where I want them." His brother's eyes were wild, darting this way and that. He had his fists up, ready to fight.

"Who you calling an asshole, asshole?"

Adam saw the first fist fly, ready to take his brother out while his head was turned, and without much thought, Adam raised his own fists and stepped right into the middle of it.

Chapter Three

Sheriff Missy Alderton was en route to Lacey's when the men all came pouring out of the pub like it was totally cool to engage in a street brawl at supper time. Pedestrians went diving for cover and cars somehow managed to avoid striking the men as they punched and kicked their way across the street.

She counted six in total. She could guess who most of them were. Four of them were likely the newcomers who were staying at Lacey's and who'd been all kinds of trouble since the moment they'd got to Grimshield. They'd been throwing their weight around, making threats — being bullies, really. There was nothing that Missy could charge them with, but she was keeping an eye on them.

The two others seemed to be the targets. They were pretty much surrounded, although the fight itself was chaotic — too chaotic for her to really see who it was. One of the targets was a big dude with huge muscles and he seemed to be holding his own, doing his best to protect the scrawnier one at his side. They were still taking hits, though, and there was blood flying everywhere.

She turned her siren on and let it go for a full thirty seconds before she skidded to a halt, turning the truck to the side to block any cars from attempting to get by. The men paused long enough to glance her way. She pulled her mic and switched over to the megaphone.

"Stop what you're doing and take two full steps away from one another." She waited a beat then added, "*Now!*"

The men, all breathing heavy, looking like they weren't anywhere close to being done, hesitated for only another few seconds before doing as she'd said. She took a lot of satisfaction in that.

"Put your hands on the backs of your heads." She put the mic down then got out of her cruiser.

Her one and only deputy, Steve Webber, was pulling up on the other side of the street. She nodded for him to get out of his cruiser and come help. He was new to the job and a little slow on the uptake.

"What do you boys think you're doing out here?" Missy said as she started toward them, her eyes darting to the big guy, his muscles bulging, his back flexing in a way that stretched his black T-shirt out beautifully. She couldn't see his face, though, and for some reason she thought he looked familiar. *Can backs look familiar? How about asses?* Because he had a fine one encased in his black fatigues. *Could bounce a quarter off those tight glutes.* His hands were threaded behind his head. His hair was cut short and a soft-looking chestnut brown. His feet were planted shoulder-width apart. Alarm bells were going off in her head all of a sudden. She knew this guy. She just didn't know how.

"Sheriff Alderton." The smarmy voice of Rex Cooper, a man she had come to know quite well, if only because of his shithead posse of men, pulled her attention away from the big guy. "I'm sorry for all this trouble."

He was walking out from Lacey's as if he had no idea how any of this had happened, when they both knew he probably had everything to do with it.

"*This* trouble?" She waved her hand around the group of men. "Is that what you mean? This bunch of adult men who were just fist-fighting in the middle of the street of my town like a bunch of hooligans?"

Rex bypassed his thugs, who were all, strangely, looking somewhat contrite as their boss handled their shit.

"Yes. They should be ashamed. There's no need for violence, ever." He pushed his sunglasses up and speared his guys with a hard look. Each of them in turn had sense enough to look ashamed. A few even turned their eyes downward, like they were searching the ground for some common sense. "I've warned them, as per our agreement, that there would be no further trouble."

"And yet, here we are," Missy drawled.

"It was one of yours who started things this time, I'm afraid," Rex countered with a glance over her shoulder.

"Not. True," a rough voice grumbled.

She felt the big guy lunge forward, and she turned, both hands up, despite the fact that her heart had kicked into high gear because she recognized that voice. "Stand down, Adam."

Holy shit! Adam fucking Lancaster was in town. Why, *why* was he back? Her throat went instantly dry as she tried, but failed, to stop herself from actually laying her hands on his massive chest. She didn't want her hands there. She wanted her hands anywhere but there.

"They threw the first punch. Tommy was just in there talking." Adam's sunglasses were still on his face, obscuring his eyes, but all the same, Missy could feel his gaze boring into her soul.

She didn't want to be standing face to face with Adam — not now, not ever.

"That simply isn't true," Rex said as he took a step closer. "Take a look around, Sheriff, it's my men who have borne the brunt of the injuries."

Missy turned around, putting her back to Adam and trying her best to calm the fuck down. She scanned the men and saw the truth of that accusation. All his men were busted up in some way — black eyes forming, lips split, abrasions all over.

"You weren't even in the room to hear what Tom was saying," Rex said to Adam. "You didn't hear him making threats against us, against me. He insinuated that he was going to slit my throat if I didn't get out of town. This from the man who owes me a considerable debt. You, whoever you are, just stepped in and started hitting my men."

"You have some nerve, Rex" — Tommy lurched forward, his fists raised — "after the threats you made to my father today? You bet I'm going to slit your — "

"Tommy!" both Missy and Adam yelled at the same time.

Adam manhandled his brother backward while Missy took a step toward Rex.

"I'm not going to arrest any of your guys this time, Rex," Missy started. "But this is your last warning."

Rex smiled in a way that made Missy's skin crawl. "Sheriff Alderton, as I've already said, my men were merely acting in self-defense and perhaps also in my honor. There's nothing illegal in that."

"Of course there is!" Missy raised her voice more than she'd intended to, but seriously, was this guy for real? "Your men are causing a public disturbance and there's no proof that this was in self-defense, especially since there were four against two. And you know this hasn't been the first incident in the time you've been here."

Rex crossed his arms. "Simple misunderstandings."

Okay, listen… You and your men —"

"No, you listen, Sheriff," Rex said as he leaned closer, his voice dropping so no one but Missy could hear. "As I've explained before, if you don't keep your people under control, I'm going to call in the rest of my family." He cocked an eyebrow. "And if you think I'm tough to deal with, you're not going to want to meet *my* brothers."

"Are you threatening me?"

"No." Rex smiled. "But I am letting you know that I'm here for a short time, doing business with some people who owe me things. If I get what I'm owed, then I'll leave. If I don't…well…then I guess Grimshield is going to experience an influx of tourists the likes of which it has never seen."

Missy opened her mouth then closed it. She knew who Rex's family was. She'd called around, done her research. Grimshield wasn't the first small town to face this attention from the Coopers, but Missy would be damned if she let her town experience the shakedown that the others had warned her about.

"So, what I'm asking for is a little bit more cooperation from you and your deputy. Please do keep your local thugs from bothering my men outside of normal business hours and this" — he waved his hand around — "kind of thing won't happen again. Now take care of these two and get them out of my sight."

He turned away and Missy had to do everything in her power not to mouth off and tell him where to go. She didn't like to be threatened, but she also didn't have any way to stop Rex from conducting his business—not yet, anyhow.

"You're just going to let him get away with this?" Adam bellowed practically in her ear. "What kind of sheriff are you?"

What the fuck did he just say? She turned to face Adam, doing everything in her power to rein in her anger so he wouldn't see it. "I'm the kind of sheriff who takes care of the local thugs." She glared up at him while speaking to her deputy. "Arrest these two and get them to the station."

"Arrest *who*?" Adam yelled, his chest expanding to the point that it almost reached her. *God, he's big.* Way bigger than she remembered.

"Adam and Tommy Lancaster, you're under arrest for public brawling and causing mischief. Turn around." She met Adam's eyes without flinching before she pulled out her handcuffs and motioned for him to turn.

He stood there, his chest heaving, his fists clenching and his body giving off all kinds of 'don't fuck with me' vibes.

"Turn. Around," Missy said through clenched teeth.

The clicking of her deputy's handcuffs on his brother seemed to snap Adam out of his testosterone-filled showdown with her. He shifted himself back then held out his wrists, a slow smile creeping over his lips.

She realized right away why.

His wrists were too big for the handcuffs. With a smile of her own, she pulled out a zip tie.

Surprisingly, he complied without another word, and within minutes, she had both brothers in the back of her patrol vehicle, one looking sullen and the other looking downright pissed — but neither bothering to argue.

* * * *

"Are you going to put us in separate cells too?" Adam growled the moment she ushered them into the station.

"I'm dropping the charges," Missy snapped. As much as she liked seeing Adam bound, she couldn't morally keep him under arrest.

"You going to be needing anything more from me right now, Sheriff?" Steve asked as he poked his head into her office, scanning both Tommy and Adam.

She waved him off. "No, I'm good."

He nodded. "I'm going to get back to organizing those old files in the basement then."

She didn't get a chance to comment on Steve's strange self-directed job of sorting through old files, because Tommy was all up in her face.

"So that was all for show?" Tommy scoffed. "Don't tell me you're scared of that guy, Missy, because — "

She pushed him back. "It's *Sheriff* Alderton, and no, I'm not scared of Rex Cooper." She unlocked Tommy's handcuffs then moved to a nearby desk, looking for something sharp to cut the tie from Adam's wrists. "But I want him to think I am."

She heard a snap and turned in time to see Adam pulling the plastic ties from his skin. "Why the hell is that?"

She shook her head. *How did he…?*

Tommy laughed. "Jesus, man, you could have snapped outta those the whole time? What the fuck are they feeding you in New York?"

Adam ignored him. "That guy, Rex whatever, is a lowlife thug. I've dealt with his kind for years. He's going to shake down everyone he can get his claws into before he leaves. Making people fear him by pulling rank on the fucking sheriff is just step one."

"Yeah, I know." Missy folded her arms and leaned against the desk behind her.

"You know? So why the fuck did you leave his guys there and arrest us?"

"Because I'm working an angle with Rex."

"An angle?" Adam mirrored her stance. Arms crossed, leaning back against the windowsill.

He looked good. Damn good. His body was tight, his thighs thick, stomach flat, and even though he wasn't wearing skin-tight clothes, she could tell that he was ripped—more ripped than he'd been that night way back at the costume party when she'd climbed on top of him and ridden him like a stallion.

She shoved her mind away from that memory, even though her mouth had actually started drooling... along with another part of her body.

"It's official sheriff's business, which I'm not going to share with you."

"*Official* sheriff's business?"

"Is there an echo in here?" She shook her head.

"You know what I do for a living, right?" Adam said. He finally shoved his sunglasses to the top of his head and his eyes were as startlingly intense as she remembered them being.

That night, so long ago, had been very damn passionate because of the look in his eyes—a one-night stand that had too much meaning for her, if only because it had been sweet, sweet revenge. But that look in his eyes, the intensity she'd seen... It had stayed with her afterward and made her want him even more.

As far as Missy was concerned, his eyes were one of the sexiest things on his entire body, and his body was pretty damn fine as it was.

Even so, she steeled herself so that she didn't flinch and didn't look away.

"Yeah, I'm quite familiar with your line of work." Who wasn't? Adam Lancaster was the right-hand man and bodyguard to the infamous Sabine Cowan—playgirl extraordinaire and a multi-millionaire on top of that. The shit he'd gotten wrapped up in because of that woman was insane. "And your line of work and my line of work don't mix well."

"Then you know that I can help you with this and that I'll get results," he said, ignoring her last comment.

"By breaking the law."

"You can't prove that."

"You sound like Rex." She knew it was a low blow and didn't regret it. Adam was exactly like Rex, throwing his weight around, trying to intimidate to get what he wanted, believing he had every right to bully his way through every situation. "I don't need your help. I've got things under control."

Adam opened his mouth but she cut him off.

"Tommy, I told you to stay away from Rex and his guys." She shifted her eyes to stare down Tommy, but he wouldn't look at her.

"They came out to the ranch this morning and threatened Dad!" Tommy attempted to shove his way past Adam but only ended up knocking himself to the side. Seriously, Adam was like a brick wall. "I had to do something."

"How much money do you owe them, Tommy?" Missy asked. The first she'd heard that there was a debt owed was when Rex had said it back on the street.

"I don't owe them nothin', *Sheriff*."

"Tommy," Adam said, his voice holding a tone of warning, "you're always getting into debt in one way or another. Answer the sheriff's question. How much do you owe?"

"Why the hell did you come back here anyway?" Tommy held his fist up at Adam, as if he could actually do some damage. "I don't need you messing up my shit. I've got things handled. Go back to New York." Tommy headed to the door without answering the question.

Adam just shook his head as he watched his brother walk away then turned to look at her once again. "You don't like my ways of doing things, fine. I promise, no more fighting. That counts for Tommy too." He raised his hands up. *Big hands. Big fingers. Strong looking.* She remembered the feel of those fingers inside her. "But you can't stop me from investigating on behalf of my family."

"Sounds like your family isn't interested in your involvement, and I for sure don't want you here." It sounded harsh, but she meant it. If Adam was around, she didn't know what crazy shit her body would convince her to do. He was bad, bad news for a girl like her, making her break all the rules when what she needed was law and order and status quo.

"My mom called me and asked for my help," Adam's tone softened. "You know it's gotta be bad for my mom to call me like that."

"Well, as you can see, I'm getting no information out of your brother. But that doesn't mean I don't have things under control. I'm running my own investigation."

"We can work together on this." Adam took a step forward.

Missy stood upright, her hands out as if she could stop him if she wanted to. *Oh, hell no!* "I'm working this *my* way. Rex Cooper and his family are connected...like crime family connected. This is the first I'm hearing about a debt, but I know when they settle in a town, they don't leave until they get what they came for. Tommy's tied up with them." She didn't elaborate, even though she could have. She knew more than she was telling Adam. Much more.

"I know guys like this, Missy. They're slippery as fuck. And you know that they aren't just going after my brother. I know you know that, so don't bother acting any other way. I can get you proof. I can get you what you need to get them out of town," Adam said. "This is something I'm good at. I feed the NYPD shit they need all the time."

Holy shit. He fed the NYPD? Like an informant? To set people up? She'd read all about the takedown of Roy Miller, CEO of Morgan and Miller. Cowan Enterprises had been all tied up in that, no doubt.

"No, Adam, under no circumstances do I want you to mess with these men. They'll call in the family, and if that happens—"

"So you *are* scared of him."

"I'm scared of his potential. I've learned what he's capable of. But I'm not scared of him." *As if.*

"Maybe you should be."

Missy's anger rose again. "Maybe you should just worry about your own business, like maybe keeping your brother from stirring up shit and messing around with my plans. He keeps coming into town piss-drunk, ranting and raving, making threats and starting fights. This isn't the first time. Soon I'm going to have to really arrest him, just to keep him out of the way."

"I'll do my best to keep my brother in check. You do your thing. We'll see where we meet in the middle." Adam gave her one last hot-as-hell once-over then turned and walked out of the door.

"There won't be a meeting in the middle!" she shouted after him, then cursed herself because, really, all she wanted was to crush herself up against him in her own version of meeting.

Chapter Four

She watched him walk away—like moved to the window to spy on him as he hustled his firm ass across the street.

But he wasn't walking right back to Lacey's... He was turning around. He was looking at her with those penetrating eyes of his. Her body flushed. *Oh fuck.* He was storming back to the office, through the door until he was in her face all over again.

And she didn't stop him. She couldn't do much more than put her hands up to his chest, just like she had in the street, but this time it wasn't to create a barrier. She needed to touch him. She needed to feel his heart thundering under her fingers.

"You can't stop me from being here." His voice was guttural, his body radiating heat. She had nowhere to go. Her butt was already pressed against the windowsill, her legs already spreading to accommodate him. He had his hands on her hips, his body as close to her as he could get with her hands on his pecs. "I've never stopped wanting you."

"I don't want you at all," she lied.

He grinned in that cocky way of his and her throat went bone dry. Her stomach fluttered around like she was once again a giddy little teenager. Adam Lancaster was staring her down with such a predatory gleam of lust in his eyes that she felt like she was going to melt into a puddle of arousal right then and there.

He lifted her, moving his hands to her ass, forcing her to wrap her legs around his waist. She had a split-second panicked thought of the possibility of her deputy walking in the room and seeing them, but that dissolved away the moment Adam latched his lips on to hers. All coherent thought left her, and her body, which had never truly stopped lusting for him, took over. He had his tongue in her, stroking her mouth, making her moan, satisfying her in a way that made her remember how it felt to have his cock buried deep. His hands on her ass moved her roughly against him so that her aching pussy rubbed against his crotch, the fabric doing nothing to dampen the feel of how hard he was under all his clothes, how huge he was. God, she remembered that cock—the feel of it filling her up, stroking her inside and out, making her moan when she rode him to climax.

Fuck, she wanted this man. She'd always wanted this man. One revenge fuck had only been enough to whet her appetite, and her attempts at avoiding him ever since had only made the craving worse.

Every part of her body was on fire. She wanted to rip his clothes off and fuck him right there on her desk. He rubbed his cock against her pussy, grinding her with their clothes between them.

She felt like it was entirely possible that she could come just from the friction alone.

She was throbbing with want and all she needed was for him to deepen their kiss, to give her space so she could move her hands and really touch him.

Then he stopped.

He pulled away from her, set her down on the floor, her legs wobbly as fuck, her breath coming out in great big embarrassing pants of desire.

He gave her a look that let her know in an instant that he was only proving a point. "You still want me."

She narrowed her eyes and crossed her shaking arms.

"If we worked this case together, we'd be close. *Really* close. All the time." Adam leaned toward her. He bit his bottom lip. "We've got unfinished business."

"G-g-et out." Missy's voice wobbled. She cleared her throat. "I never want to see you again." Words she'd said to him years ago when he'd tried to call her after the party. Words she hadn't meant then and didn't mean now.

Adam stared down at her, the cocky smirk gone, as if her last words had wiped it away. "Suit yourself."

This time he walked out and didn't look back.

Missy collapsed to the side, her whole body shaking as she tried to regain her composure. *Holy shit! What just happened?* The very thing she'd fantasized about for years? Adam Lancaster was back in town and all she wanted was to fuck his brains out—that, or arrest him again.

Despite the fact that this was a fantasy come true, she didn't have time for this shit. Adam being back in town complicated things, in a big way. Not just because of her sexual infatuation with him, but also because he had a notoriously shady way of dealing with situations.

She ran her hand over her face and sighed. She'd have to figure out a way around the man. *Probably easier said than done.*

The pieces of zip tie that Adam had busted were at her feet. She bent down to pick them up, marveling at how clean the edges were. The man was huge, sure, but there shouldn't have been any way he could snap that zip tie.

She pulled the two remaining ones from the pouch on her utility belt and tried to stretch them. They were solid, no notches or weaknesses that she could see.

She moved to the hallway where the open door to the basement let a distinctly musty smell invade her nostrils. "Steve, you still down there?"

They couldn't seem to keep deputies in Grimshield. Steve was number four and she wasn't sure he was cut out for police work. He seemed perpetually scared — ready to jump at the slightest noise — and he also seemed to be able to do a whole lot of nothing on his shifts, even though he appeared to be working hard at something all the time. She could hear him rummaging around, probably making more of a mess than he was supposedly cleaning.

"Yeah, boss?" He poked his head around the corner, a box in his hands and dust on his face.

"Do me a favor and check over all the zip ties. See if there are any in there that are broken or notched or something."

"Notched?"

"One of the prisoners was able to snap the tie right off. I want to know how he did it. There must be something faulty with the ties."

"He did *what*?"

Missy rubbed her hand over her face. She'd always considered Adam Lancaster to be the kind of guy who could do anything, even in the times that she hated his guts. He was impressive, and not just because of his body. His mind was sharp and he'd always been a fixer, helping people when they needed it, solving problems when they arose. She hated to admit it right now, but she'd always admired him.

Revenge fuck or not, the truth of the matter was that she hadn't stopped thinking about him and his glorious cock in all the time he'd been gone.

"He snapped it in two." She held up the broken pieces for Steve to see. "I don't care how big he is. He shouldn't have been able to do that."

Steve trudged up the stairs, reaching for the pieces once he hit the top step. "Huh, that's weird."

Yeah, duh! Missy bit her tongue rather than snap at the poor fool.

"Not sure how'd he'd be able to do that." Steve rubbed the back of his neck.

"So investigate it. Figure out how he did it and let me know."

Steve snapped his eyes to meet hers, probably wondering if she was mad at him, something he used to ask her every thirty seconds when he'd first started. She'd straightened him out right quick. *'I'm not mad at you, usually, I'm just…well…mad in general.'* What she was mad about, she wasn't totally sure most of the time. Missy was just irritated with people, things, disorder, how unfair life was…

"Sure thing, boss." He didn't wait for further direction. He just tilted his hat a bit then turned and went back into the basement.

Missy walked to her office and closed the door. She needed a vacation—a nice long vacation on a desert island...with Adam. *No! Not* with Adam. She sighed. Her mind was a traitor and so was her body. The memory of Adam was infused into her very soul. She moved to her desk and turned on her computer. The damn thing was old and clunky, but it still worked in the ways she needed it to, albeit slowly.

As she waited for it to boot up, she let her mind scroll back through her history of Adam Lancaster, lusting and longing—first to that night when she'd dressed up in her best friend's super-sexy angel costume then had somehow worked up the nerve to leave the house in it. That entire night had been so out of character for her, but she'd been young, just turned twenty-two, and she'd heard that Adam was back in town for a few nights. She'd known he'd be at that party, and she'd had something to prove. No matter how self-conscious she had felt, something had compelled her to go, and once she'd arrived there and had seen him all dressed up like a pirate, looking his usual smug but sexy self, well...she'd decided what she had to do.

He hadn't known it was her. Not at any point had he suspected that the sexy-as-sin dark angel who'd climbed on his lap and had ridden him to climax was the very same girl that he'd said such mean things to ten years earlier.

How could he? She'd grown up and had put on some weight in all the places that guys seemed to crave. She had tits and an ass and hips that she had known would look so good in that costume. Since the last time he'd seen her, she'd really transformed. And by the glint in his eyes all those nights ago, she had known that he'd liked what he'd seen.

She'd had her vindication, not only in the fact that he couldn't keep his hands off her, when his body had responded in just the way she'd wanted and when he'd come so hard that he had looked like he was in heaven. He'd said things to her too, that night. He'd looked her in the eyes and told her that she was the most gorgeous creature he'd ever seen, and he'd tried to get her to stay, to take off her mask and tell him her name. Then she'd leaned in really close and had told him exactly who she was.

The memory of that night gave her a cascading rush of giddiness. She'd accomplished something that she hadn't thought possible. She'd banged her greatest conquest. And when he'd practically begged her to see him again, she'd had the ultimate satisfaction of telling him no.

Adam Lancaster, the guy who'd treated her like she was nothing but a nuisance when she was younger... The guy who, one balmy summer day almost ten years before that night, had told her that no guy was ever going to want to date her if she didn't quit the tomboy act and clean herself up. That day all those years ago, Adam had crushed her young heart by basically telling her that she'd never be good enough for a guy like him. He'd called her an ugly duckling like he was doing her a favor. She'd never forgive him for that, no matter how much revenge she got.

Well, she'd proven him wrong, hadn't she? *Ugly duckling? Ha!* She'd given him a night he apparently hadn't forgotten.

She sighed again. Problem was, it was a night she hadn't forgotten either.

Her computer finally loaded and she clicked the Internet browser. She'd done this search so many times that she didn't know why she bothered doing it again — but all the same... She typed Adam's name into the search bar and waited for it to load the hundreds of thousands of hits. There were always so many. She'd read stories about how crazy the paparazzi where when it came to Sabine Cowan and, by extension, Adam. She'd even read about how one photographer had waded into crocodile-infested waters to get a picture of Sabine at a closed golf course.

The computer finally loaded.

Adam Lancaster, Arrested for...

Adam Lancaster, Bodyguard to Playgirl Sabine Cowan...

Adam Lancaster, Head of Security...

Adam Lancaster, Sexiest Man Alive...

He sure was. She clicked on images and watched as photos loaded featuring many different versions of Adam. He looked good, no matter what he was wearing — a suit, jeans, a pirate costume. Yeah, the man was hot as hell and she wanted more. She'd always want more. But he was also kind of a jerk and definitely played a little too close to the wrong side of the law. He'd been arrested too many times for her comfort, if she believed the media, which she did. And he'd been accused of even more nefarious shit over the years. He'd proven over and over to the world at large that he'd do just about anything for his boss, the gorgeous Sabine Cowan.

Of course Missy was jealous. Sabine was successful and rich. She was also too beautiful to be real, with a body to die for. Rumor had it that she and Adam were a thing — a sexual thing for sure and likely much more than that. Missy had had one night with Adam. Sabine had him every day and night.

Missy would say she didn't approve, that she didn't like the life that Adam seemed to lead with the sex parties and Kitty Cat girls all around him, but in reality, everything about Adam intrigued Missy — always had, always would, not that he'd ever know about it.

Soo-o, yeah, Missy didn't like Adam being around as a reminder of something she couldn't have. That night at the party had been a one-time thing meant to prove to herself that she could get a guy like Adam. But it would not be repeated. *Uh-uh, no way.*

She squirmed in her chair, her thoughts going to the feel of his chest. He was solid, a wall of muscle. And he smelled good, like 'she wanted to eat him up' good. There was a little clove or spice to his scent that made her mouth water. And his eyes when he'd taken those sunglasses off had been just as she always remembered — dark, deep blue and so intense that she felt stripped down from the inside out. That kiss was enough to fuel her fantasies for days. The man was trouble, and not just because she kinda wanted to shake his hand for beating up Rex's boys. He was trouble for her. One wrong move and she was sure to cave to his sexy body, just as she almost had today.

She didn't want him getting in the way of her investigation. Rex Cooper and his men were only a small problem compared to the rest of his 'family'. She wanted to take care of that problem before it turned into something too big for her to handle. She'd called some law enforcement buddies she had — a couple of guys who'd had dealings with Rex Cooper and fam — and they'd given her some really good information. She'd never catch Rex in the act, not unless she was smart and strategic. And she needed to catch him doing something really bad to get him to move on. So far, every interaction she'd had with the man somehow turned into some kind of bizarre police harassment scenario where he twisted things to make it look like *she* was the one causing problems, not him. Added to that was the county commissioner's involvement.

Not only had Commissioner Richardson drastically limited her ability to police, with all of his budget cuts in the last few months, but he'd interfered twice now on Rex's behalf, siding with the man and almost going so far as to accuse Missy of misconduct.

If only Tommy Lancaster would unzip his lips and tell her what the fuck was going on, like what was *really* going on. There was something deeper happening there. She could feel it.

If she could convince Tommy to wire up, she'd be able to get Rex making threats — then she'd have something. But like she'd told Adam, Tommy had so far refused to give her anything. He wanted to handle this his way, and now that his brother was back in town, Missy was worried that things were about to get totally out of control, which also had her worried that her attempt to keep things professional between her and Adam would be impossible.

Chapter Five

Of course Adam had known Missy Alderton was sheriff now. But actually seeing her in her snug-fitting uniform with all her curves, her hair pulled back into a ponytail that was all business... Well, he just hadn't been able to control himself.

He also didn't believe for one hot second that she wasn't just as into him as he was into her. Sure, she hated his guts still, but that didn't mean they couldn't work that rage out between the sheets...against the wall, from behind with her hands splayed on her desk...

Right. She was hot. *Super fucking hot.* It was a far cry from the days way back when she had been all gangly and awkward.

That day he'd last need Missy all those years ago, he'd been searching for a quiet spot to think. He and his dad had just gotten into it something fierce. Adam had been out of school for a year, working on the ranch, training the horses—freeloading, as his dad liked to say. A buddy of his had told him about a job coming up for private security, basically a babysitting gig for some rich dude in New York. His buddy was committed elsewhere, but he hadn't wanted the job to go to waste, so he'd reached out to Adam, knowing he had an interest. Adam had thought it was a great opportunity to get out of Grimshield, that maybe putting some distance between his dad and him would help or something. His dad hadn't seen it that way. For all his comments about Adam freeloading, he'd flipped the fuck out when Adam had told him he'd accepted the security job that would take him to New York. He'd told Adam that he was abandoning his family and leaving his old man to do the hard work of keeping the ranch alive.

Talk about mixed messages.

Adam had gone out to the river that day, pissed off and wanting to think it all through, maybe give his buddy a call to make sure the job was the real deal. The last thing he'd wanted was company. So when Missy had showed up all scruffy and sullen, as she normally was back then, poking and prodding at him about why he was sulking all alone, he'd snapped a bit. He'd said a few not-nice things, maybe suggested she go take a bath. That was harsh but not untrue. Back then, she had been a tomboy through and through. Her hair had always been matted and her clothes usually covered in grime. She hadn't exactly cared much about her appearance.

He'd called her an ugly duckling. Thinking back on it, yeah, he felt bad. He'd meant to motivate her, to let her know that under all the dirt and grime he knew she was gorgeous. Well, he'd motived her all right...motivated her right into one hell of a vendetta, not that he'd minded her method of getting revenge. It was just that…well, he liked her…like *really* liked her.

The Missy he'd seen today was full of confidence and fiery resolve. Everything he'd admired about her when she was just a kid was still there, except now she was also super fucking hot and all-the-more intriguing to him. And he'd never stopped lusting for her after that night at the Halloween party. No matter what happened in his life, he always reflected back on that one night with Missy and how much he wanted more.

Sure, he'd been angry when she'd arrested him and Tommy, making him think that she was under the thumb of that thug Rex, but once Adam realized that she had a game in play, he'd understood. Rex would underestimate her because she was a woman. He'd seen it time and time again with Sabine as she'd clawed her way to the top, becoming one of the most influential CEOs in New York's sex industry, among other things. Missy had the same attitude—calculated and full of sass. It made him want her even more.

He never could keep things simple, and with Missy, things were definitely complicated.

Adam was just getting close to Lacey's when he realized he couldn't actually go inside now. *Fuck!* His plans to stay away from his parents' ranch had been totally derailed as soon as he'd gotten involved in that fight. No way he could stay in his rented room at the hotel with Rex and his guys there. That would likely compromise Missy's investigation somehow, which he didn't want to do.

All the same, he wouldn't give up his room at Lacey's just yet. He'd pay her for the night and more, if necessary, just to keep it available. *Never know when a spare room might come in handy.*

With a sigh, he redirected so he could cut into Lacey's parking lot from the back and grab his rental. He'd have to figure out a way to get the duffel he'd dropped during the fight later, because it wasn't on the front porch where he'd left it. Lacey had likely hauled it inside for safekeeping. Good thing he'd left his laptop in the SUV.

He needed to get settled for the night so he could do some research on Rex and his boys. If he was going to help Missy with her investigation on the down-low then he'd need to put some plays in motion that would give him access to insider information. Yeah, Missy wouldn't be too happy with his methods, he was pretty sure, but what she didn't know wouldn't kill her.

He'd worry about how he'd convince Missy to let him help later. She was stubborn, but she couldn't be impenetrable to his charm, no matter how much she hated him.

He smiled to himself as he climbed into the SUV. *Piece of cake.*

* * * *

He was expecting to walk in on a full-blown family dinner with his dad, brother and mom seated at the kitchen table with maybe a ranch hand or two. What he found was his mom, sitting alone, nursing a tea and looking years older than she had the last time he'd seen her.

"Where is everybody?" Adam said as he opened the screen door.

Not that he minded having his mom to himself, but still... He'd been geared up for a full-out word war with his dad, so he was amped and bouncing a little.

"Oh, Adam, you came!" His mom looked up from her tea, her eyes red-rimmed, and that gave his heart a thud.

His mom didn't cry.

She hastily wiped her cheeks then rose. He had her in his arms within seconds, giving her the biggest bear hug he could manage without crushing her. She smelled as she always did — a little bit of sunshine, a little bit of grass, maybe a bit of laundry in there too. She smelled like home.

"I missed you," she said into his chest.

"I've missed you too, Mom." And he had, more than he could actually say. Moving away from home then staying away had been one of the hardest decisions of his life...if only because of her.

"Let me look at you." She pulled back and lifted her hands to his shoulders. "Look at all these muscles! Adam, I think you're twice as big as you were the last time I saw you!"

Adam grinned. "I put a lot of time in at the gym these days." He was also living clean — no booze, no drugs. After a very serious near-miss with the law and possibly also death years before, he'd made a promise to himself and to Sabine that he'd stay clean. He put all his energy into working out, and that meant his body looked pretty pumped up most of the time.

"You look good. Healthy." She smiled up at him, her eyes crinkling in that way she had that let him know she was truly happy in the moment.

"I feel good."

She ran her hand down his arm, then noticed his knuckles, which were messed up a bit from the fight. She lifted his hand to examine the cuts. "What happened?"

He shook his hand free. No sense in lying to her. "Got into it with some of those guys in town."

"Oh, Adam!" She covered her mouth.

"Tommy was mouthing off at them and making threats. They went to cold-cock him and I stepped in."

"Where's Tommy now?"

"Don't know. He left the sheriff's office—"

"The sheriff's office!" She slumped back down to her seat.

"Mom, calm down. It's okay." He crouched down next to her and put his hand on her leg. "Seriously, nobody was hurt." *At least nobody who didn't deserve it.* "And Tommy and I are okay."

His mother blew out a long breath and tried for a weak smile. "You don't know what's been going on here."

He shook his head then shifted so he could sit on the chair to her left. "I don't, but I'm here now, so you can tell me everything."

"You should get some ice on that hand." She started to rise.

Adam put his hand on her arm. "Don't worry about it, Mom. Sit. Tell me what's been going on."

She looked like she was going to argue with him over the ice, but when he shook his head again, she relented and melted back into her chair.

"Tom disappeared for a while," she started, then patted Adam's hand when he looked confused. "I didn't want to worry you."

"Mom, I—"

"You have a life in the city, Adam. I don't expect you to come running every time Tom has an issue."

Adam had in the beginning, after he'd settled his life and gotten himself out of trouble. He'd come running a couple of times until his dad had made sure he knew he wasn't welcome.

"He was gone for a year. He'd leave messages sporadically before that but then he just vanished. We informed Sheriff Alderton and she looked into it, got a trail on Tom and figured out that he was down south. Mexico. She called in some favors to get information and made sure that Tom was alive. And he was, living it up at a resort, not a care in the world, not a care for his old mom and dad. That was for sure."

Adam snorted. He didn't have to say it. They were both thinking it. *So typical of Tommy.* His mom loved both her boys — there was no question — but she was sick of Tommy's shit as much as Adam was. The only person who seemed to see the best in Tommy was Adam's dad. Unconditionally.

"So we were angry. Yes, even your dad was mad. Hard to imagine, I know." She sighed. "Eventually, we moved on with life, feeling better because we knew he was safe. Time passed. We had tabs on him through the Sheriff's connections. Then a month ago he just showed up. Out of the blue, he's back home and he's got himself in a tizzy." She took another sip of her tea. "Oh, dear, I didn't even ask you if you wanted some. I'll make another pot." She started to get up but Adam stopped her.

"No, Mom, sit, I'll do it." He patted her hand and she smiled.

"Thank you, dear."

He kissed her cheek before moving over to the counter where the kettle sat. "Keep talking. I'm listening."

"So, yes, Tom was all worked up, gushing on about how he could get us a great deal on the ranch, enough money for us to retire in style, he said. Wanted us to move to Mexico with him. Even had the nerve to tell us what a great life he'd been living down there. He said we were getting too old to manage this place, and he isn't wrong, but we weren't considering selling, not anytime soon. Tommy was persistent and adamant that we needed to sell and get out of town."

Adam filled the kettle then put it on the stove to heat up. "Let me guess. The buyer is someone connected to Rex Cooper?"

"Oh, that vile man? Yes, I suppose so. I wasn't there for all the talks that Tom and your dad were having. It was like Tom was having some kind of mental breakdown or something. Any time he sat down with me, he'd be talking a mile a minute and going on and on about what a great life we'd have if we just got out of this town. He wouldn't listen to a thing I had to say about it, avoided answering questions directly and really just wouldn't stop pestering."

Adam grabbed two tea bags and dropped them in the teapot. It sounded like his brother was on something. When Adam had been living his worst life, he'd been snorting speed like crazy and all his conversations had been on hyperdrive because his brain was constantly working at super-speed. It wouldn't have shocked Adam to learn that Tommy was into some heavy stuff, above and beyond the booze.

"Anyway, that went on for a couple of weeks, and the more we said no, the more frenzied Tom seemed to get. I'd catch him on the phone at all hours, whispering in that angry way of his. You know how he gets."

It sounded to Adam like Tommy had made a promise to someone that he'd get his parents to sell the ranch and was panicking that it hadn't worked out.

The kettle started to whistle. Adam took it off the burner then poured the hot water into the teapot. He carried the pot over with a mug for himself and set everything down on the table.

"That's when we started hearing about these guys who'd come into town, staying at Lacey's and causing problems. They showed up around the same time that Tom came home."

That was no surprise to Adam. He knew Tommy was neck deep in some kind of shit with Cooper and his guys. Things were starting to piece together. Rex had said that Tommy owed money. Maybe the ranch was collateral in some way.

"Tom broke down one night after I asked him what was going on. I mean, what was *really* going on." She gave Adam the look that said she'd laid it on thick for Tommy. If there was a pro at the guilt trip, it was her. She'd perfected it over the years. Back when Adam had been a teenager, all she'd had to do was give *that* look and he'd blurt out whatever it was he'd done wrong. "And he told me that he owed those guys a lot of money, and the only way he could get out of it was if he convinced us to sell the ranch."

"Son of a —"

His mother cut him a hard look.

He lowered his eyes. "Sorry, Mom."

"I know how you feel. Tom's gone and screwed up something awful and now he's brought us into the mess with him. Believe me, I feel the same. If it were up to me —" She squeezed her lips shut and shook her head.

"Dad wanted to bail him out, right?"

She blew out a long breath. "Offered to sell some of the stallions. Try to drum up what he owed. But he said it wouldn't be enough, then he let it slip that it wasn't money the men are after. It's the property itself." She reached over and poured the tea. "Then that thug Rex and his men came here this morning and they started making threats. Your dad got carried away and made threats back." She put the teapot down with a thud. "And here we are."

"Where's Dad?"

"He's out in the barn helping a mare birth a foal. He's got Dr. Rose, the new vet, there with him."

"And Tommy hasn't been around tonight?"

She waved her hand, a look of disgust flashing on her face—there and gone in an instant. "He'll turn up. He always does. Probably off licking his wounds with one of the girls he likes to hang out with." She clucked her tongue at that. "If you two got into it with that Rex fella and his goons, he'll likely lie low for a while. Come home after midnight stinking drunk, no doubt." Then she paused and her eyes grew wide. "You don't think they'll do anything to him, do ya? The ones you fought with?"

Adam thought back to the fight and the words that had been blurted out afterward by Rex. "No, I don't. But if Tommy's not home by midnight, I'll go out looking for him."

His mom nodded and curled her fingers around his. "I don't know what he's gotten himself into, but this time I don't think we're going to be able to bail him out, no matter what your dad says. These guys are bad news, and Tommy is in over his head."

Adam squeezed his mom's hand then picked up his mug and gulped down most of the tea. "Missy's working on an investigation of her own. I'll get to work as soon as I get to the loft."

"It's *Sheriff* Alderton, Adam," his mom scolded. "Don't act so familiar with her. She works hard for us and she deserves respect."

"Aw, Mom, you know I don't mean any disrespect. I'm just used to things being a little less formal back in the city." He had a few detectives on speed dial in New York, and he was on a first name basis with all of them.

"Well, you aren't in the city right now, so check yourself, if you don't mind." She lifted her chin and gave him a pointed look.

"Yes, ma'am."

"Now, get those clothes off. I'm doin' laundry and I don't have a full load." She stood, her hand out expectantly.

Adam barked a laugh. "These are the only clothes I have right now. I left my duffel bag outside Lacey's. And I'm not wearing boxers."

"Yes, and you're covered in dust and dirt." His mom frowned, lifting her finger to her lips like that would help her problem solve. "Well, strip down anyway. You're going to need fresh clothes. I'll go get you some of your dad's shorts to wear."

Adam pushed his chair back and stood. "Mom, come on. I'm not going to fit into dad's clothes."

"You're not sassin' me, are ya?" She motioned with her hand. "Take the clothes off. I'll get you a towel to wrap around yourself. You can go straight up to the loft and have a shower. I'll bring the clothes up when they're done." She started walking away then added, "You hungry? Likely you are. I'll fix you up some food before you go."

And that was that. He was going to have to strip down to his birthday suit. Luckily, the ranch was pretty much off the grid. No paparazzi would be snapping shots of Adam hanging out in a towel while his mom washed his clothes.

Chapter Six

Good lord, is Adam wearing nothin' but a towel?

Missy's headlights skimmed right over him as she turned her truck into a spot near the house. Why was Adam outside holding a plate of food and wearing nothing much to cover up that glorious body? It was a crime in progress for sure.

She needed to turn around and leave. Instead she sat in her truck, her eyes on the steering wheel, taking a few breaths to get her body under control. She wanted to stare at him. She wanted to lick him, actually...from top to bottom.

Get a grip, Missy!

There was a knock on her window. She jumped. Adam was standing right outside. She scanned his chest, which seemed impossibly huge and so thick with muscles that she could weep. She cleared her throat then rolled the window down.

"Adam."

"Missy." He had a cocky grin on his face, like he knew just how much he was unnerving her. "You come here to sit in your truck and admire the view — or for some other reason?"

Her cheeks heated.

He held up his plate. It was piled with mashed potatoes, meatloaf and some veggies. The smell was heavenly. "Mom'll make you up a plate."

Missy's stomach growled. She opened her mouth to decline, but he didn't stand around waiting for her to answer.

She watched him walk away and felt a tug to follow him, as if she were leashed to him. That man's back was just as sexy as his front. He had actual dimples at the base of his spine, just above his ass. *Good Lord! How did he get such a glorious body?* And that towel... She was wishing hard that that towel would just shake loose and fall to the ground. She could stare at that ass all day.

It felt like a losing battle. Her unending lust for the guy who was only supposed to be a one-night revenge fuck was completely consuming her. Maybe she should let it.

Wait...what? No. She couldn't let that happen. *No way.* And yet her eyes kept going back to his body again and again.

With a sigh she killed the engine, pulled Adam's duffel bag from the passenger seat and got out. She could have sent her deputy to deliver the bag, but when Lacey had called the office to let her know Adam's stuff was still there, Missy hadn't hesitated for even a second. She said she'd be right over to get it. Then she'd gone home, had a shower, put on her tightest, most flattering jeans and a button-up shirt that didn't cover her cleavage, and had driven straight to the Lancaster ranch. There hadn't been much thought involved. She was drawn to him, like she'd always been, for her whole damn life.

She walked around the side of her truck to see Adam settling in on the porch at the little table that was there. "I'm not here for long." She lifted the duffel. "Just bringing this by for Lacey."

Adam grinned. His legs were apart and he was leaning back in the chair. If she shifted her eyes ever so slightly, she'd be able to see his —

"Oh yeah? Well, Mom's already putting food on a plate for you, so you're going to have to stay. Plus, your stomach sounds like it needs something." He motioned to the seat across from him.

She really didn't want to stay — but she also really, really wanted to stay.

Fuck this man!

Yes, yes, I think I will.

No, stop! He's not on the menu.

Ever again.

Suuure, he's not.

She climbed the three steps of the porch and put the bag down. "Looks like you're outta clothes."

His grin widened. "Mom's washing mine. But yeah, thanks. That saves me a trip to Lacey's later."

"You weren't seriously going to go back there, were you?"

He picked up his fork and scooped up some potato. "Sure was." He shrugged. "I've got a room booked there."

"Adam —"

"Hey, let's not talk about work. Sit." He motioned to the chair again.

Work was the only safe topic where Adam was concerned. "Okay, fine, so tell me… How'd you get out of that zip tie?" She motioned to his chest. "I get that you're big and strong, but you shouldn't have been able to break that thing."

He winked, his grin firmly in place. "Sit down and I'll tell ya."

"I'm not here to socialize." But she also couldn't stop her eyes from roving all over his body. Like seriously, the man was sculpted in ways that made her mouth water.

"Sheriff Alderton!" Adam's mom, Sally, said cheerfully through the screen door. "So good to see you again." She had a plate loaded with food in one hand and utensils in the other. "Sit and share a meal with Adam."

Missy opened the door so Adam's mom could come out. "Thanks, Sally." There was no use fighting it. The smell of the food was making her stomach go bonkers and she really did want to sit down with Adam, if only to stare at him a little more. "You know you can call me Missy."

"I like calling you sheriff. You earned your title. I'll bring out some wine—"

"Oh no, water's fine." Missy took the offered plate. "I may have to go into work later tonight."

"Oh, that's a shame." Then she caught sight of Adam and her eyes went wide. "You're sitting there in a towel? I thought I told you to go find a housecoat in the loft!"

Adam grinned. "I was on my way, but Missy showed up. She brought my duffel bag with my clothes."

"Thank God for that!" Sally shook her head. "I almost get the impression he'd rather be naked anyway." She laughed.

Missy smiled for her benefit. Knowing what she did about Adam's lifestyle, he probably spent a lot of time naked, especially since there were always amazingly hot women surrounding him. "I'm only looking at his face and didn't even notice he wasn't wearing clothes."

Adam snorted. Sally winked. And Missy tried hard not to blush...again.

"Well, I'll leave you two alone then. You've probably got things to discuss." She gave Adam a look that seemed loaded.

Adam waved her away with a slight shake of his head.

Sally left without another word, but she did give Missy a pointed look before the door closed behind her.

"What things do we have to discuss?" Missy set her plate down, doing her best to ignore Adam's bare chest. It wasn't often a big guy like Adam had no chest hair. Did he wax? Was it natural? How soft was his skin...because it looked pretty freakin' soft. And his shoulders... His arms... Actually, those forearms were something else too. He could probably curl an impressive amount. She could imagine what those forearms would feel like wrapped around her breasts, caging her in as he was drilling her from behind. *Whoa...wait! What's going on here?* Her face felt hot again. She lowered her head, thanking her past self for leaving her hair down so she could shield her growing embarrassment. She really needed to get a grip and stop staring.

"No work talk tonight, remember?" He was half finished with his plate. "Eat."

Missy didn't take well to orders, but she was hungry, plus the food was distracting. She cut a piece of meatloaf. She couldn't remember the last time she'd eaten a home-cooked meal.

"How are your folks?"

She frowned. *Mood effectively killed.* The radiant heat from her cheeks cooled in an instant. He didn't know. Of course, why would he? He hadn't been around and, she reminded herself, it wasn't like they were friends. "They passed actually." She cleared her throat and hurried to add, "About four years ago now."

"I'm sorry, Missy." Adam sounded sincere. "I didn't hear about that. Mom and I have a sort of agreement that we don't talk about anything that might bring me back."

Missy's frown deepened. Why wouldn't he want to come back? Better yet, why would the death of her parents make him want to come back? "I wouldn't have expected that from you. The funeral was very small, just family." Just her actually, since her mom and dad had been the only family she had left. Her heart gave a hard thud and she resisted the urge to reach up and rub away the flash of pain. It still hurt something awful after all these years. With her parents dead, she felt very alone most of the time, like an orphan with no blood relatives left.

He reached over and touched her hand. "All the same, I'm sorry for your loss."

Appalled that his gesture actually made tears burn the backs of her eyes, Missy yanked her hand back and got busy cutting her meat up into very small bites. "Mom died in her sleep. An aneurysm. Dad went a few months later. Cancer." They'd worked their whole lives right up until their deaths, always travelling so far just so that Missy would have a house and food and later an education. She'd stayed with them, took over paying the bills and tried to make their lives easier once she was employed, but it never seemed to matter. Dad hadn't liked to sit idle and Mom had always been worried about a rainy day. After they died, Missy discovered that they'd hoarded a small fortune. Lots of money, sure, but she'd give anything to have her parents home all the times they hadn't been over the years. She'd spent so much time alone, fumbling through life events by herself. She'd give all the money back if it meant they could have lived a while longer.

"That's rough." He cleared his throat. "Bet they were so proud of your accomplishments, though, right?"

Missy smiled at the memory of her dad's beaming face and her mom's enthusiastic cheer when she had crossed the stage at graduation. "Yeah, they were. They weren't too keen on my running for the sheriff job when it came up, but they knew I always had a thing for following the law and keeping everything in order."

Adam's eyebrows shot up. Something else he didn't know about her. She was all about rules. She didn't like coloring outside the lines, which was why she wasn't too keen on having Adam around. Not only did he mess up her hormones completely, but he was notorious for breaking the rules.

"And how are things here? I mean, when there isn't a gang of guys starting a street fight?"

She'd been expecting some kind of jab about arresting him, but when she snapped her eyes up from her plate, he was giving her a lopsided grin.

"I'm not sorry," she blurted, "about arresting you."

"I wouldn't expect you to be. You were always trying to prove a point when you were a kid. You had the perfect opportunity today to show me how tough you are." He continued to smile.

"That's so patronizing," she scoffed. "You haven't really changed much, have you?" She shoved a piece of meatloaf into her mouth.

He leaned back, grin still in place, and crossed his arms. His ab muscles flexed and Missy had a hard time swallowing her food. Those muscles of his cut down into a perfectly tantalizing vee that went right past the towel and made her think of all the ways she could trace that line with her body, her fingers, tongue...

"Neither have you, is all I'm saying."

She put her fork and knife down. "I didn't ask you to come here, Adam." Why did her voice crack when she said that? "I've got things under control. I know all about you and your ways of fixing problems. I've read the articles about your boss and about Cowan Enterprises."

"And let me guess, you don't approve," he drawled, clearly not bothered by her words.

"Why would I approve?" All the jealous feelings she had rose. All the biases did too. "You work with a woman who exploits other women. What's there to approve of?"

Adam's eyes went wide again and he sat upright. "Sabine doesn't exploit any of the Kitty Cats."

"The Kitty Cats?" she scoffed. "Seriously? You can sit there and say in the same breath that she doesn't exploit women but she calls them Kitty Cats?"

"She's in the sex industry, Missy. The women who work for Cowan Enterprises understand that sexualizing the brand in all possible ways helps the company be as successful as it is. No one is there against their will, and believe me when I say that the women are treated very well and are generously compensated."

Missy crossed her arms and rolled her eyes. "That's what all you people say, playing innocent when really the girls are forced into—"

"Hang on there." Adam raised his hand. "Like I said, nobody is forced into anything and I'm surprised, and a little hurt actually, that you'd think I would work for a company that allowed it to happen. I might have moved away, but I didn't become a different person. It's like you think I'm some kind of villain."

Missy winced but covered it up quickly. "The media—"

"Has their own version of everything. You should know that. They've demonized Sabine for decades, but I promise you that not one of our employees is treated unfairly. Sabine makes sure they fully consent to all practices they participate in and are compensated generously. She makes sure they're educated and that they have a Plan B for after their time with the company. She empowers the women who work for her."

Missy had never heard this version of things, nor would she ever assume that Sabine's sex-focused company would do anything but exploit the women employed. Everything Adam was saying went against what she'd read…or seen…or imagined…

"I'd be happy to give you a tour one day, let you talk to some of the Kitty Cats yourself."

Missy was shaking her head before he could finish speaking. "Uh, no. Thanks." That was definitely not on her list of things to do with Adam.

"Well, if it isn't my eldest, returned to save the day."

Missy turned toward the sound of Denny Lancaster's sarcastic voice. He was walking up the path from the barn with Dr. Rose at his side. Both men's clothes were disheveled and covered in blood and mucus. She'd heard there was a mare foaling and that the vet had been up there since noon. Not much happened in Grimshield that she didn't know about.

"Hi, Dad," Adam said gruffly.

"Sheriff Alderton, wasn't expecting to see you back here today."

"Good evening, Denny." Missy stood, suddenly feeling awkward. "I came by to bring Adam his clothes."

Denny's eyes went wide. "Seems like you failed in that mission, huh, Sheriff?" He was smirking at Dr. Rose, who was snickering as well.

Missy felt her face burn, but she pointed to the duffel bag. "He left his stuff at Lacey's."

"For shame, son, sitting there in a towel with a woman present," Denny said. "Honestly, you'd think this boy wasn't raised right with the way he carries on. Such an embarrassment." He turned and shook hands with Dr. Rose. "Thank you, sir. Your services were invaluable today. Send me the bill and I'll bring a bank note."

Missy shot a look Adam's way. She'd heard Denny speak that way before about Adam but never in his presence. Her earlier judgment of Adam sat heavy on her now, especially considering the expression he had on his face…like he wasn't surprised to be so publicly belittled. All families had issues, but she firmly believed that those issues were not for an audience.

"My pleasure, Denny. That foal is a beauty. Glad I was able to bring him into the world without much trouble."

Missy picked up her plate and busied herself with getting the dishes inside. There was a cloud of unease and she knew it was time to go. Adam was right behind her, but he didn't follow her into the kitchen.

Sally was busy washing dishes. "Oh, hon, you can put that right there." She pointed to the counter. "You have enough to eat?"

"I did. Thank you. It was delicious."

"I hope there's some left for me," Denny grumbled as he walked into the kitchen and got ready to plop himself down at the table.

"Oh no you don't!" Sally turned on him. "You get yourself upstairs and clean yourself up before you get a bite of food."

Missy was expecting Denny to snap back but was surprised to see him trudge out of the kitchen.

"You're not leaving because of him, are you?" Sally sighed. "His bark is worse than his bite."

His bark was pretty bad. "No, no, I have to head home and get some sleep in case I get called in later."

"Well, you never do know what those awful men might do at Lacey's," Sally said as she scraped Missy's plate clean.

"Give me a few days and I'll know exactly what they're doing at all hours," Adam said as he walked into the kitchen, fully clothed, head-to-toe in black.

She was about to ask what that meant when he added, "I apologize, Sheriff, for being underdressed. It was rude."

Missy felt his sudden formality like a slap.

Denny grunted as he entered the kitchen again. "Damn right it was."

"Well, you didn't have any clothes to wear," Missy said. "Glad I got a chance to help you out there." She offered a smile.

Denny had changed his shirt and his hair was damp. He caught the sharp look Sally gave him and had the sense to soften his tone. "I got this out of the laundry room. Washed up in there. I'm starving, Sal."

Sally *tsked* but handed him a loaded plate all the same.

"Thanks for sharing a meal with me. It isn't often I have someone to talk to over dinner." Missy shifted her eyes away from Adam's and nodded toward Sally then her husband. "Thank you for the hospitality."

"Any time, Sheriff," Denny called after her as she beelined for the door.

She had only ever known love and respect from her parents. They hadn't been around as much as she would have liked, but they would never have treated her the way Adam's dad had just treated him.

Maybe that was the reason why he'd left Grimshield in the first place—and why he never seemed to want to come back.

She frowned. Maybe she didn't know Adam Lancaster as well as she thought she did.

Chapter Seven

Missy couldn't get Adam out of her head.

She was all hot and bothered, so much so that as soon as she got home she went straight for another shower to cool off.

To cool off. Yeah, right.

The water was beating against her sensitive skin, touching her in all the places she wanted Adam to touch her. Her mind kept going to him in that towel and how she would have liked things to go if the circumstances had been different. Like, if they'd been alone and if she didn't hate him.

Okay, that was a lie. She didn't hate him. She was just very, very frustrated by him.

What was there not to be frustrated by? He was sexy as sin and trouble with a capital T. She couldn't get him out of her head. His voice. His scent. The feel of his chest. All those hard muscles.

She shuddered.

So yeah, she was in the shower and her mind was wandering to all the things she wished had happened between her and Adam.

She slipped one hand down her stomach to her pussy and moved the other hand to circle her nipples, then she let her dirty thoughts take over.

Adam in his towel. His glorious body on display.

"You come here to sit in your truck and admire the view or for some other reason?"

"I came here for you," Missy purred as she jumped out of her truck and got right in his face. "I came here to tell you what I think of you. What I really think of you."

"Oh yeah?" Adam got in close, pushing her back until her ass hit the side of her truck. His smell was up her nose, in her mouth, making her drool, making her melt. "So tell me, then." His words were husky and she could feel his cock pressing against her belly, rock hard and ready for her. "Tell me how you really feel, Missy."

The way he said her name, like he wanted to eat her alive, was just about all she could take. She kissed him then, roughly, without mercy, her hands on his body, running her fingers along his chest, and his hands were on her, pulling at her clothes, so that they could be skin-on-skin.

He was so big, his body dwarfing hers as he lifted her up, gripping her ass but not breaking their kiss. Tongues still probing, hands still roving, he carried her into the barn.

He stripped her clothes off in a frenzy and tore his towel away. There he was, naked, his body like a sculpture, so magnificent and that dick… Oh boy…he was going to fuck her so good.

He took her in, his hot stare making her wet, then he pushed her up against the wall, her arms pinned above her head, his lips on her nipple, sucking, flicking, teasing. She wanted this, a quick and dirty fuck, and he didn't disappoint.

He pushed her legs apart with his knee, wedging himself in so his cock pressed against her pussy, tormenting her with the proximity.

"You want me. Don't lie, Missy. I know you do." His voice was gruff, his cock just there, ready to slip inside.

She opened her eyes, looked at him, staring into his intensity and nodded.

He didn't release her hands, his grip firm and locking her in place. With his other hand, he held her hip. She lifted her legs to wrap around his waist.

"I want you…always have," she admitted.

His stare blasted her, looking dangerous, and he wedged his big, fat dick deep inside.

That was all she needed. She could imagine the feel of his cock stretching her. She remembered how big he was, how hard he'd gotten when they'd had sex all those years ago. As she stroked herself to her climax, she swore she could feel the ghost of his dick pounding her pussy, just as he had that night so long ago.

"Fuu-uck," she sighed as her orgasm crashed through her, making her throb, making her moan.

How she was going to survive this man being around she didn't know, but she sure as shit couldn't spend all her time masturbating to get him out of her system. She'd never leave her house if she did.

At least that took the edge off…mostly.

She got herself dry, dressed and made some tea. It wasn't like she hadn't been fantasizing about Adam for years now. Or that she hasn't been stalking him online in all that time, thinking up different scenarios with him. The difference now was that he was in town. He was actually in her face, blasting her with everything that was Adam — his smell, that spicy scent of his that made her mouth water and her body zing, his voice, so gruff and masculine. He was very commanding, not just in his size but in how he carried himself and how he spoke to people. She liked that. It turned her on.

She was in way too deep already and nothing had actually happened between them.

It wasn't just that he liked to walk around nearly naked, teasing her with his gorgeous body. It was all the other stuff too. For years her opinion about Adam hadn't changed. He'd been a jerk to her when she had been younger. He'd said shitty things to her way back then. She'd wanted revenge. But now, after seeing how his family treated him? Well, she had the niggling gut feeling that Adam was used to hearing insults and negative comments when he was at home. The way he'd reacted—or actually, how he hadn't reacted— made her realize that his family, maybe with the exception of his mom, didn't actually want him to be there.

She knew Tommy and Adam had issues. *But what brothers don't?* She hadn't known that Denny Lancaster held such animosity—enough to openly express it, even with company over.

It made her want to give Adam a hug, which was weird considering all she'd ever fantasized about was possibly licking him from head to toe and riding him like a bucking bull—nothing at all related to romance or loving on the guy. Had she been objectifying him all these years, never really considering him as a thinking, feeling man?

Maybe.

Yeah, definitely. For all her judgment of Sabine's company and her apparently mistaken understanding of how she treated her Kitty Cats, Missy wasn't really any better than Adam's father.

Witnessing Denny's harsh attitude toward his elder son that night had made Missy realize that there were layers to Adam that she'd never really known. And it made her soften toward him in a way that was confusing.

All she knew about Adam came from her past, maybe jaded experience with him and whatever the media had put out there about his lifestyle in the city. It wasn't a complete story.

"Adam's back in town," she said when her best friend Tori picked up on the first ring.

"Whoa, hello there! You mean Adam-the-guy-you've-been-in-love-with-your-whole-life? That guy?"

"I'm *not* in love with him!"

Tori scoffed. "Okay, so you're in lust with him. Have you jumped his bones yet? Gone for round two?"

Tori was the only other person who knew what Missy had done. She'd been part of the revenge planning when Missy had found out Adam was back in town that night so many years before. And, really, Tori had been the one daring Missy into doing it, giving her the pep talk that had finally pushed her out of the door in that hardly there costume.

"No!" When he'd been sitting there on the porch, outside his family's home, practically naked, she'd had a lot of things going through her mind, but telling him that she hadn't really stopped lusting for him wasn't one of them. Besides, she didn't have to admit that out loud. He knew.

"You know, if you tell him that you forgive him for being an ass all those years ago, it'll get all the awkward shit out of the way and you guys can get right back to business. And by business, I mean fucking."

"Tor! That's not what I want to happen."

Tori's laugh echoed loudly in Missy's ear.

"I'm serious!"

"Seriously infatuated with the guy." Tori chuckled again.

"You're not helping."

"Okay, so what's the problem? If you don't want to be around him, then avoid the guy."

"That's the problem. He's in town to help his family with a situation going on here, and even though I've told him to stay out of my investigation, he won't listen."

"So arrest him for obstruction or whatever."

Missy snorted. "Been there, done that." And she was still dying to know how he'd broken through that zip tie.

"You *arrested* him?" Tori gasped.

"He was fighting in the street and I needed to send a message, so yeah, I did."

"Wow, way to assert yourself, lady! High-five! You're awesome!" She paused. "So you still love-hate him then, right?"

"I don't love him! How many times do I have to tell you that?" Missy sighed. "I'm infatuated, fine. I can't get him out of my head. He's driving me crazy because he's hotter, if that's even possible, than I remember, and he's also…well…maybe not exactly the asshole I remember him to be." Okay, he wasn't at all the asshole she remembered. It was possible her memory of their last encounter — the one before the party — was skewed by her puberty-fogged brain and a touchy, overly sensitive reaction to the truth.

Tori didn't say anything right away, and that didn't help Missy's whirling thoughts.

If she were going to be honest, Missy had always been intrigued by everything about Adam, even from the time she had been a kid. She'd looked up to him at first, then, once her hormones had kicked in, had wanted his attention more than anything. She'd hung around pestering him when he had been down by the river or when he'd been walking into town. She'd showed up at the bush parties, even though she had never been invited and had certainly been too young to be welcome. She'd sought him out whenever she could, but she'd never really gotten to know him. Her main goal had been to just be near him, so she could stare and fill up her fantasy fodder for later.

"It sounds to me like you've got an itch to scratch with this guy," Tori finally said.

"An itch to scratch?"

"Yeah, like you can't get him out of your head, so maybe you should do something about it. Satisfy that urge."

Fingering herself over a fantasy definitely didn't compare to the real thing. "You mean seduce him?"

"Damn right! Show him who's in control. Maybe bring the handcuffs too."

"I can't do that!" Missy's cheeks were suddenly on fire.

"Why not? You've done it before with this guy, and I'm not just talking handcuffs. You fucked his brains out, remember?"

"Yeah, but that was different." She'd done that for revenge. She'd wanted to prove that she could get a guy like Adam after what he'd said to her. She was now just realizing how petty that had been. Not that she thought he minded what happened between them that night, but now, with things getting complicated, she feared that if she started something with him, she wouldn't be able to stop herself from doing it again and again. There was a definite addictive quality about Adam that Missy didn't want to explore.

"How so?"

"I was wearing a costume that night, totally in disguise, and it was only meant to be a one-time thing." Tori didn't need to know about all the other feelings she was having. Feelings that just made everything so foggy—feelings that might prove to Tori that maybe Missy was a little bit in love with Adam.

"So...wear the costume again. It was a one-time thing five years ago. Make it a one-time thing again now. Then you'll get him out of your head and he'll be left a drooling mess. You're an empowered, sexy-as-fuck woman, Missy. Take charge and get what you want."

Missy laughed. *As if.* "The man has been seduced by better, I'm sure."

"Why, because he's Adam Lancaster, the sexiest bodyguard alive? Isn't that what that magazine called him? Or because he works for the gorgeous woman, Sabine what's-her-name? You think you can't compare with her? Is your paranoid brain making you believe that you're not good enough again?"

"Ouch, no!" *Yes!*

"You know I'm right. You're always playing down your talents. You constantly underestimate how fucking fabulous you look and undermine the bad-ass bitch that you are. It never makes sense to me why you wouldn't be feeling in control. You're hot, lady. You know he's going to be all in, especially if you put that sexy angel costume back on."

"This is such a bad idea." So why was she actually glancing toward the closet where she knew the costume was hanging?

"Is it, though?"

She needed him out of her head, needed to get her lust under control. Maybe this was the way to do it. One more time with Adam, then she'd be satisfied.

Terrible idea, Missy.

"This is a fabulous idea, Missy. I'm telling you. Put that costume back on and scratch that itch. Then your head will be clear and you can take care of the issues you're having in your town. Sex works wonders for head clearing. Trust me. I know."

That, Missy knew, was the understatement of the century.

Chapter Eight

Adam's security team back home had done some dark web digging and had gotten contact information for Rex and a few of his men. It was all Adam had needed to send a Trojan virus in the form of super-sexy videos that he knew those guys wouldn't be able to resist. He now had access to all the devices that Rex and his men had on them. If there was one thing he knew very well from working with Sabine, it was that men could not deny their vices. Predictably, they'd clicked the porn link and had given Adam full access.

He'd accessed the cameras to take a peek and turned the sound on so he could listen. His computer was running a program that would capture still images and video as well as record audio for however long he was connected. It would be a lot of data to sift through, but his team back home was on it.

He'd done the same with Tommy, but instead of sending a Trojan to access his device, Adam had sent one to get a tracker on him. He wanted to know where his brother was at all times. Right now, Tommy was staying put at a house in town that was owned by one of his old girlfriends. *Also predictable.*

Adam was lying in bed and it was late, but he was too wired to sleep. The loft was above the garage and completely separate from the main house. It was cozy and his mom had decorated it to suit her tastes since he'd left home. From the time that he had been about twelve until he'd moved to New York, the loft had been his room and sanctuary, but now it was all baby blues and soft yellows, with paintings of flowers and horses. There was a shelf in the corner with a pile of romance books and no motherfuckin' TV, so he was left with nothing to distract him from his thoughts but a whole bunch of older lady stuff.

He grabbed his phone from the bedside table and was about to launch one of the games on there that he never used — that was how bored he was — when he heard the telltale creak of someone coming up the stairs. He was up and nearly at the door when the light knock came.

Expecting his mom, he flung the door open wide and was nearly knocked over by who he saw.

"Missy?" He squinted into the limited light. "Is everything all right?" Her hair was piled up into a sexy, messy bun at the top of her head and she was wearing a lot of makeup, more than she had been earlier — and ruby-red lipstick that reminded him of...

He took a step backward when she moved inside, closing the door behind her. Her hands were on his chest a moment later and she pushed him back until his legs hit the side of the bed.

She didn't say a word, but her eyes were all hooded and Adam's heart started hammering because he could tell that she wasn't there for a conversation.

She unbuttoned the long jacket she was wearing with one hand while she pulled something out of her pocket with the other.

All the feelings Adam had from the one night so long ago came back in a rush. She slipped the mask from his memories over her face...then let her jacket drop to the floor. Adam's racing heart went into overdrive and his cock — *Fuck, man* — was so instantly hard that it hurt.

"You are so fucking hot," his voice came out in a croak.

Missy didn't say anything. She didn't have to.

This was the Missy who had blown his lusty brain to bits — his naughty angel, the one he hadn't stopped thinking about since that night at the party. She wasn't Missy the sheriff, not right now.

"Where are your wings?" It was meant to be a joke, to get her to smile, but it seemed she had other plans.

She climbed onto his lap, forcing him to lie back a little as she straddled him. He put his hands on her ass and helped her to shove the tight skirt up so that her bare pussy was on display.

Her *bare* pussy! This was straight out of his fantasies.

All further jokes slipped out of his brain, along with all coherent thought. He growled. She lowered herself to his lap and rocked a little, her lips curled into a smile that could actually kill him.

"You said that night that you wanted a round two." Her voice was husky.

He could hardly believe this was happening. "I did! I've wanted this for a long time. I've never stopped thinking of you, Missy. I — "

But she didn't let him finish. She stole his next words with a brutal kiss. Darting her tongue deep into his mouth, she rubbed her pussy against his cloth-covered dick and all he could think about was getting inside her...but first... *Fuck...* First he wanted to taste her.

He slipped his hand between her legs, rubbing her soaking wet pussy, slipping between her lips until she was moaning into his mouth and rocking her hips so that he'd hit her clit in a steady rhythm.

There were so many things he'd fantasized about doing with her, so many times he'd jacked off to the idea of those things. Now that he had her, he wasn't going to waste his time.

"I want to eat you," he growled on an explosion of breath.

She gasped, her head back, her breasts jutting and barely covered by the halter-top she was wearing. God, he wanted to rip all her clothes off and pound into her something fierce. But she was moving down his body, her hands gliding over his chest to his boxers then directly clasping his aching dick.

She didn't give him a chance to think or to react beyond a deep, guttural moan as she pulled his cock out of his boxers and sucked him down hard and fast, taking him into her warm, wet mouth all the way until he hit the back of her throat. Her lipstick was smudged, her mouth stretched open wide and her eyes were locked on his.

He dropped his head back, holding position with his elbows somehow bracing his upper body. She cupped his balls with one hand and sucked him off with her mouth. It felt like fucking heaven.

He wanted this so badly. His balls were tight and he felt like he could come right down her throat any second and —

She stopped…like dead stopped. The weight shifted from the bed. Cold air hit his cock and he lifted his head in a daze, his eyes only half open. Missy was gone.

"Missy?" he croaked. *Fuck, did I imagine it all?* Not like this wouldn't be the first time a fantasy dream of Missy had felt so real.

He rolled to his side and there she was, busy looking for something in her jacket.

"What are you — ?"

She held up a condom and slipped it onto the mattress before standing up.

"I told you I want a taste." Ignoring the condom for now, even though he badly wanted to pound into her, he reached out and gripped her hip then pulled her to the bed. She was way smaller than him and weighed nothing, so it wasn't anything to flip her over and spread her wide so he could kiss his way up her thigh and straight to her glistening pussy.

She tasted glorious. Like honey… No…like…he didn't even know what she tasted like…just sweet and delicious. "You taste so fucking good, Missy." He licked and slurped, and rolled his tongue over her clit. He'd wanted to taste her and suck her juice down his throat, but no matter how much he'd fantasized, nothing compared to the real thing. There was no way he'd get enough just from one night. There was no getting this woman out of his system. He'd known that for years.

He nipped her clit lightly then sucked her hard until she was writhing and bucking, and he knew she was ready to explode. He hooked his fingers deep inside and rubbed her G-spot, and she nearly jumped right off the bed. God, she was so fucking sexy. The way she moaned, the way she moved… *Ahhhhh, man, she is* so *hot.*

She arched her back and cried out. He lifted his head for a second to watch her tear at her halter, yanking the zipper down so that her perky tits were out, her nipples budded and rosy.

She clasped onto the pink buds and rolled them between her fingers and thumbs, and he resumed sucking hard on her clit, giving her what she needed to push her over the edge. She pumped her hips against his mouth and he watched her orgasm hit. He felt the steady pulse of her coming and heard a deep, unhinged moan that was music to his ears—just like all those years ago.

Now…now he could fuck her sweet cunt.

"Take that skirt off. I want to see you naked, baby." The skirt had ridden up around her waist, giving him full access to her pussy, but he wanted skin-on-skin. He wanted her bare.

He whipped his boxers off and grabbed the condom. She was panting, her eyes bright, her chest and neck flushed. She didn't take the mask off, and he liked that. But she did unzip the skirt and wiggle herself out of it. Her tits jiggled in the process and he couldn't help himself. He reached out to stroke her nipples, giving a bit of a pinch because those hard little beads were just too tantalizing. He couldn't wait to suck them harder and fill his mouth.

He slipped the condom onto his cock, which was primed and ready to explode, then gripped her ankle before she could move away from him. He pulled her closer so he could grab her hips and turn her around. Her glorious ass was nudging his thighs, the perfect heart shape with the tightest-looking puckered hole.

Fuck he'd love to pound his cock in between those cheeks, but not tonight. He'd save that for the next time. Right now he just wanted to fuck her pussy proper.

She spread her knees and lifted her ass, looking at him over her shoulder with her sexy lips curled into a daring smile, and he just couldn't hold off for a second longer. He gripped her hips and plunged in deep, so deep that his balls smacked the top of her pussy and her entire body shifted up the bed.

Her tight pussy gripped him so good that his dick pulsed and he almost lost his load right then and there. But he held on, pulled himself back out then rammed her again—and she took it. *Holy fuck.* She took it with pretty little moans coming out of her mouth and her tits swaying. It felt so damn good.

He wanted to drill her over and over, but he also didn't want to come too fast, so with a gigantic effort, he slowed himself down and got himself under control. Closing his eyes to reset his brain, he rolled his hips and rocked into her more gently, getting into a rhythm that was more of a tease, a slow stroking, and her keening moan was music to his ears.

When he opened his eyes again, the sight of her body swaying forward, her head down, her hands splayed in front of her to keep herself upright... Well, it was beautiful to behold. His fantasies couldn't even compete with the reality of this scene. It was too fucking intense for his imagination. Too perfect, too.

Keeping one hand on her hip, he reached forward with the other hand so he could cup her tit. He liked the feel of her flesh in his hand. He loved how her tightly budded nipple rubbed against his palm. Her skin was so warm, her body so fucking hot.

He moved his hand down so he could pinch her nipple, and she groaned in response, so he did it again—pinched and rolled it between his finger and thumb. She rocked her hips back, pushing against him hard, encouraging him to move faster, to go harder, deeper.

Of course he would oblige.

She turned her head to watch him over her shoulder. There was a spark in her eyes. Then she curled her lips into a wicked grin and said, "What are you doing back there? Napping?"

Adam smiled back. *Oh hell no!* Challenge accepted.

He moved his hand back to her hip, lifted her up and rammed her hard—so much so that she lost her hold and slid down to her face, her head nearly pounding against the headboard.

It took only three strokes to get her pussy clenching onto him tightly, spasming all along his shaft, and once she started to come, he couldn't hold back. His balls were so tight, his dick so stiff, and he bellowed as jets of hot cum filled the condom.

It was a never-ending rolling wave of pure bliss, the best orgasm of his life. Better even than the first time they'd fucked.

Seriously.

There was no way he was letting this girl slip from his grasp again, and he definitely wasn't through with her tonight.

Chapter Nine

Adam woke up with the best sex hangover he'd ever had—and the biggest shock of his life, Missy wasn't gone. She was in the loft, using the bathroom. She hadn't cut and run. And that made him feel…well… great actually.

He could smell her all over his bed. She was all over his body too. He lifted his fingers to his nose. Her scent was so fucking tantalizing. And last night—*holy fuck*—it had been spectacular. After five years of lusting, of fantasizing, he'd had all his depraved dreams come true.

"I want to tie you up." The second she came out of the bathroom, she was on him, straddling him, his cock just barely touching her pussy and all he wanted to do was grab her hips and ram her onto him.

He snorted. "Tie me up with *what*?" If she was going to say zip ties, he was going to say 'hell no'. Even though he had his ways of getting out of those things under normal circumstances, he wouldn't be able to do it now, not when he was buck naked and horny as hell.

With a sly look on her gorgeous face, she slipped off his legs and moved to the side of the bed where her jacket was lying on the floor. Within seconds she had two long red strips of cloth in her hand and was holding them up triumphantly.

Adam lifted his arms and spread them out to the sides, giving her an answer without having to say a word. She got busy wrapping his wrists and tying one at a time to the thick bedposts. Once she was done, he gave a tug and grunted his approval. She'd done a good job. The knots were tight enough to hold him in place but not tight enough to ramp up his anxiety at being confined. Bondage play was okay with him and he could totally indulge Missy's sexy fantasies like this, but he needed to know that there was a way out.

Missy slid onto the bed from the side, just at his chest. The mask she'd been wearing earlier was gone and her cheeks were a pretty shade of pink. Her eyes were riveted to his body, so he flexed his muscles, knowing full well how good he looked splayed out like this.

Her eyes went wide. She licked her lips. He could see the hunger there, staring back at him. His cock pulsed, bobbing almost painfully with his excitement. He wanted her to touch him. To kiss him. To ride him already!

She leaned in closer, so close that he could feel her breath skimming across his sensitive skin. *Touch me! Lick me! Kiss me!* Her eyes were locked on his. A small smile played on her lips but she didn't touch him, not even when she lifted her hand and traced the cut of his muscles. Her fingers didn't make contact. They skimmed just above. He jolted all the same. It was like he could feel the electrical pulse of her almost-touch, as if her energy was bridging the gap she was creating with her maddening actions.

"Missy," he growled and tugged at the bonds, making the bedposts creak and letting her know that he could bust out of this game of hers at any moment.

She snapped her eyes to his at the same time as she straddled his legs. "Don't you dare," she growled back.

She reached over him to the bedside table to grab a condom then ripped open the package slowly, teasing him with the promise of what was to come. He pushed his hips up, his dick bobbling in front of her. She grinned at him as she rolled the condom on, and even that slight touch was enough to get his body revving even harder.

She flattened her hands on his torso, her fingers splayed, her pussy high enough that he couldn't yet feel its heat. Then she leaned forward until her lips were hovering just over his. He wanted to reach up, to capture her in a brutal kiss, but he didn't. This was obviously her fantasy. He didn't want to ruin it by taking control.

"Adam," she whispered. Her voice was husky, her breath coming out in gusty bursts. She slipped her hands around his body and brushed her tits along his chest. Instant jolts of lust zapped through him. His nipples hardened at the feel of hers.

She pressed her lips to his and slid her pussy right onto his cock. His brain misfired instantly. All his muscles went taut, his arms straining against the bonds. He groaned into her mouth, and when she pulled herself back, she had that cunning little smile on her face once again.

She moved her body slowly, tantalizingly so, like she was dancing to a song only she could hear. He wanted to run his hands along the smooth contours of her hips, up her long waist to her tits, and as if she could read his mind, that was exactly what she did now. She ran her fingers up her body until she got to her breasts, which she circled slowly, pinching her nipples at the same time that she arched her back. His cock was throbbing inside her, the condom driving him mad. He wanted to be bare, to really feel her, but he knew that kind of trust would have to come with time. And he wanted time with Missy. He wanted all the time in the world.

She closed her eyes as she rolled her hips. Watching her grinding into him so slowly, her perfect body moving so smoothly, revved him up hard and fast. He bucked up, using his core strength to pump her pussy. Her eyes flew open and locked on his. She leaned forward, placing her hands on his abs, and met his pace, pound for pound. Within minutes they were both moaning. Adam's orgasm exploded through his entire body like a freight train full of cum. He filled that condom good.

And that wasn't the last of their fucking either. After they'd caught their breath, Missy removed the bindings and they went at it again.

So yeah, Adam's body was sore in all the right ways. And he was in such a damn great mood when Missy slipped out to go home that his mother's invitation to join the family at breakfast didn't seem like such a bad idea. Fuck, after his marathon sex night and morning with Missy, everything seemed like a wonderful idea.

In fact, he couldn't keep the damn grin off his face as he walked to the house. The morning was crisp. The birds were chirping. The horses were neighing and Adam felt like he could accomplish anything.

Missy...*fuck*. She blew his mind. He couldn't wait to see her again—to have a chance to talk, to catch up for real and get to know one another as adults without all the posturing and bullshit. *Shit*, he didn't even have her number.

"What's the whore's boy doing here?" Tommy grumbled into his coffee as Adam stepped into the kitchen.

And just like that, Adam's mood shifted. *Bubble effectively burst.* He tempered his anger, trying not to let Tommy stoke his fire.

"The prodigal son returned to beg forgiveness," his father said as he came into the kitchen on the opposite side. "Gonna fix everything up for us, he is."

"Denny," Adam's mom snapped, "enough of that." She grabbed a plate and started loading up some eggs. "I asked Adam to come home so he can straighten things out with those men. He has expertise in that area. He'll be able to fix this."

"He'll do what?" Tommy and his father said at the same time, both looking at her like she'd grown another head.

"You've lost your minds, I tell ya." His mother didn't stop what she was doing. She just continued to load up a plate, shaking her head slightly as if she were dealing with a bunch of morons. "Tommy, you come in here stumbling around drunk, ranting and raving that you've got things under control, then piss yourself on the couch... You're telling me you've got this under control? And Denny, you're too damn old to do any good in this situation. With all your blistering and blustering about it, you'll likely have a heart attack and leave me to manage this place all by myself."

"Sally, don't say shit like that," his father said, his tone softer. He avoided eye contact with Adam but did look a little sheepish as he took his seat and waited to be served.

Mom had that power over everyone. She could make someone feel like shit with just a look and have them begging for forgiveness with a few words.

Adam moved to her side and started to load up the next plate, giving her a hand so they could all be seated while the food was still hot. She nudged his arm in thanks when he took two plates over to the table and set them down in front of Tommy and his dad.

Neither thanked him, not that he expected them to.

His mother brought his plate and her own and finally they were all seated. The table felt really small all of a sudden.

"Tom, you're going to tell us what's really going on," their mother said. "No more lying." She raised her fork at him when he started to argue and she stabbed the air. "And don't you tell me that you've got it under control, because you don't."

Tommy glared at Adam. "I would have had it under control if this asshole hadn't stepped in and cause all kinds of trouble yesterday."

"Language, Tom!"

Tommy dropped his eyes to his plate. "I'm sorry, Ma, but seriously, he came in there and threw his weight around and now Rex is threatening to bring his family here too."

"The way I heard it, you were about to get your ass whooped and Adam stepped in to keep that from happening," their mother said.

"Tell him to bring his family. We can take 'em."

"Denny." Their mother rolled her eyes.

"I don't think he's talking about extended family here, Dad." Adam set his fork down. "I've done some research."

"Of course you have," Tommy drawled, crossing his arms.

"Rex means family as in crime family." Adam nailed Tommy with a hard look. "That's what was going on while you were in Mexico, right? When you disappeared and had Mom worried all those months?"

"Like you've never worried Mom. Let's not forget your stint in rehab—"

"Enough, boys!" their father roared, startling everyone at the table with the ferocity of it. "Tommy, is that right? You brought some kind of Mexican gang down on us?"

"Not Mexican—and not a gang." Tommy's face was flushed. "I didn't know they were connected. I met Rex at a party and he convinced me to join him for an extended vacation. I didn't know where we were going or who I was with."

"For a year, Tom?" His mother was shaking her head. "For a year you were partying with these men and you didn't get a hint that they were trouble?"

"Oh, he knew they were trouble." Adam pulled out his phone and flicked through the photos he'd gathered, showing Tommy doing things that would make their mother gasp…then cry…maybe also smack Tommy around for being such a blazing idiot. Drugs, sex… Tommy had done it and documented it. Ironically, there wasn't a whole lotta difference between Tommy's life and what Adam's had used to be—the past that Tommy and their dad couldn't seem to move beyond. But where Adam had evolved and put an end to his publicly partying ways, but Tommy seemed to just be ramping up. "You can find just about anything on the dark web."

Tommy's eyes were wide and he was leaning forward, looking about ready to snatch Adam's phone if given the chance.

Adam found the picture he was looking for and turned it so Tommy could see. "You wanna tell us who this is? Keep in mind that I already know."

Their mother took the phone and squinted at the photo before passing it to her husband. "He looks like a drug dealer."

Elton Morrow was, indeed, a drug dealer—one of the most notorious for slipping through the cracks in more than one way. He was on so many watch lists that it was awe-inspiring, but no one could get anything on the guy—not for lack of trying.

"I've only ever met him once, I swear," Tommy whined.

Their father studied the picture and scoffed. "He doesn't look like much."

"And you could take him," their mother finished for him. "This is what I'm talking about. You're going to get yourself killed."

"And Adam is supposed to stop that from happening?" His father snorted, giving Adam a good once-over. "Just because he's as big as a house—"

"No, because he's good at what he does."

"And what's that exactly?" Tommy snarled. "Chasing after women? Doing your boss's bidding? Surrounding himself with filth. All those sluts—"

Adam pushed his chair back and pointed his finger toward Tommy. "Watch how you talk about my boss and my colleagues." He took his phone out of his father's hand. "You're one to talk about hanging out with filth." Adam waved his phone as a reminder of what he had on it, then slipped it into his pocket. "You don't want me here. I get that. But Mom does and I'm not leaving until I've helped you two get rid of these guys. Missy" — he coughed — "Sheriff Alderton is doing things her way and I'm doing things my way. Together we'll find something we can use against these thugs."

"You can't use the information on your phone?" His mother waved her hand toward him. "This man he associates with being a crime lord or whatever you called him?"

"Not unless he actually makes an appearance and does something to break the law." Adam shook his head. "And the sheriff isn't exactly keen on my methods."

"Because they're illegal, no doubt," Tommy said.

"I use what tools are available to get the job done and maybe bend the laws a little." Adam shrugged. "It's not like we're dealing with stand-up citizens. Right, Tommy? I've got other pictures here. You want to see them?" He started to pull his phone out of his pocket and smiled. "Then we can really talk about breaking the law."

Tommy's face flushed and he pushed his chair back. "I'm not going to sit here and listen to this."

Their father took that cue was well, shoved more food into his mouth then grabbed his coffee. "I'm with you, Tom." He followed Tommy out of the front door.

Adam surveyed the table with a feeling of disgust. "Sorry, Mom. You shouldn't have to put up with this."

His mom leaned into him, putting her head on his chest and wrapping her arms around him...or tried to, anyway. "You always were a good boy. We can't help who we're related to." She laughed.

He smiled and squeezed her back gently. "I'll help you clean this mess up."

"Oh no you don't." She lifted her head to look up at him. "You've got important work to do. I didn't call you here for dish duty." She patted his chest then pushed herself away. "I've got all morning to clean this up. You get into town and do what needs to be done."

Adam nodded. "I'd like to go and speak to Sheriff Alderton again." *Among other things.* "And let her know what I've found out."

His mom paused, one hand stretched out to grab a plate, the other on a glass. The look she gave him made him pause too. "Oh, honey, you sure you want to fill her in on your methods? She is the sheriff, after all."

Adam smiled. "Don't worry, Mom, I know how to talk to women like Missy. It won't be a problem at all. She'll see my way is the best way."

Chapter Ten

"You did *what*?" Missy blurted, hardly able to contain her frustration with this man. "Do you have any idea how illegal that is?" He'd gone and done exactly what she didn't want him to do. He'd used some kind of techno spyware something or other to infiltrate Rex Cooper and his men without their knowledge, totally breaking the law and violating their privacy.

Not to mention she wanted to jump him so she could ravish his body again...which was also very frustrating. *One more time, my ass.* Her addiction was full-blown now. She could wring Tori's neck for convincing her that going over to his place the past night had been a good idea.

She hadn't stopped thinking about Adam all morning. In fact, she couldn't get that tantalizing smell of his out of her nose or the feel of his body against hers from her memory. They'd had an explosive night *and* morning and now her body craved him...like she actually felt herself swaying toward him as she stood trying her best to keep the glare on her face.

"With connections like these guys have, I'd think you'd want to know what was going on in their rooms."

"You could compromise my entire investigation." She wasn't going to lie. Spying on these guys could yield some very useful information — none of which she could act on or use against them if she wanted to press charges.

"You're overreacting."

"Did you seriously just tell me I'm overreacting?" She gave him another glare, trying not to sweep his body with lust instead. Last night had been so hot and so much of what she needed. He'd touched her in all the right ways. He'd let her play out so many of her fantasies. Tying him up? Oh yeah, that had always been her number one go-to, and the reality had not disappointed her in any way. Seeing his huge body bound and splayed, his muscles straining... Well, even the thought of it now made her all hot and bothered.

He'd fucked her so good that her pussy was still buzzing from it and her head was struggling to stay in the game.

He moved closer to her, a cocky grin on his face. "Yeah, I did. What're you going to do about it?" He had her crowded against her desk, her ass hitting the edge. The heat radiating off him made her want to move in closer, wrap her arms around his waist and kiss his neck.

Normal couple behavior.

Her whole body reacted to him. She breathed in his scent, letting it soak deeper into her psyche. He was wearing all black and his eyes were so intense that she wanted to flinch, to pull away. But she also wanted to grab him, push him onto her desk and climb on top of him so she could rub herself all over his body.

They were alone in her office. Steve, her deputy, was out dealing with a domestic call. All she had to do was lock her office door and — "Can you back up please?" Her tone was more curt than she'd wanted it to be, but all the same, this couldn't go on. Last night was only meant to be a release, not an awakening.

The smile faded from Adam's lips. He was looking at her in a way that suggested he was waiting for a punch line. When it didn't come, he took a few steps back, his hands up. "Sure, no problem."

Oh, she liked that. Adam taking orders. She liked that a lot.

The sight of him, his hands up, doing as she demanded, snapped something inside her, some kind of restraint she had. It was suddenly gone.

She pulled a zip tie from her utility belt and wrapped it around his wrists before he could do much more than flinch.

"You arresting me again, Sheriff?" His voice was a low rumble that sent shivers through her body.

She loved that hooded look to his eyes, the way he bit his bottom lip.

"I want to see you get out of this. I want to know how you did it."

His lips spread into a cocky smile. "You'll have to torture me for that secret."

She moved past him to the door and turned the lock. "That will not be a problem." She couldn't help herself. She needed this to happen…again.

She moved to the window and tightened the blinds then flicked the lamp on her desk so that a soft glow of light cascaded over everything. She wasn't going for romantic. She just wanted to see what she was doing—who she was doing—because part of the appeal of fucking Adam was looking at him while she did it.

The man was a god and she wanted him.

"Lean back." She motioned to her desk and watched with satisfaction as Adam did as he was told, positioning himself so that his bulky body was leaning more than standing. "Put your hands behind your head." Again, he did as he was told. She loved the way his T-shirt strained against his biceps. "Now don't move a muscle." She plopped down onto her wheelie chair and moved closer to him. No sense in busting up her knees when she had the right kind of equipment around.

Adam adjusted his stance, widening his legs, leaning more on the desk.

Missy flicked her eyes up to meet this just as she put her hands on his thighs. "I mean it. Don't move."

"Yes, ma'am," Adam grunted.

Good boy. Missy couldn't help a grin from spreading. Fuck, she was wet. Just the idea of sucking Adam off, right here, right now? Well, it did incredible things to her body. She might actually come just from touching him.

The man was intoxicating.

A definite addiction.

She couldn't get enough.

She rubbed her palm over the bulge in his pants. He had the biggest dick she'd ever seen, rivalling some of the porn she'd watched over the years. He was hard, growing harder as she moved her hand along his shaft. "You've been naughty, haven't you?"

Adam grunted again.

She moved her fingers to the zipper. "You want me to take it out?"

He nodded, the muscles in his arms straining as he held his position in the zip ties.

She curled her fingers over the button of his jeans and popped it open, then moved to nub of his zipper and tugged gently, teasing him with her pace.

"Missy," he groaned.

"Yes, Adam?" she continued to move the zipper in a painfully slow way. Her body was trembling with anticipation. She could see his flesh and realized he wasn't wearing any boxers. She had to squeeze her legs to keep herself from rocking on her chair.

"I'm dying here."

She glanced up at him and saw the truth of that statement written all over his face. One last tug and his cock was free. She thought about teasing him more by pulling his pants to his ankles, but the sight of his dick made her impatient and she couldn't help herself. With his dick in her palm, she leaned in and ran her tongue from base to tip.

And was rewarded with the most guttural-sounding moan she'd ever heard.

It was all the encouragement she needed. She rolled her lips over his cockhead, sucking back the pre-cum that seeped into her mouth, and used her tongue to flick his most sensitive parts as she moved herself down his shaft. His dick was definitely a mouthful, and her lips were stretched almost to the point of pain, but she kept going, taking him in as far as she dared, right to the back of her throat—and he still wasn't completely covered.

He moaned again, a rumble of sound that made her shiver. She cupped his balls with one hand, and as she moved her mouth back up, used her other hand to wrap around his shaft so that she could rub him at the same time as she sucked him.

She felt his hands on her head, pushing her down so she could pump him faster. She tore herself free, his dick hovering just at her lips. "I said keep your hands behind your head!" She growled and snapped her eyes to meet his.

He was smiling in a lazy kind of way, a quirk of his lips and a glint in his eyes that let Missy know he was only going to indulge her for a little bit longer. "Yes. Ma'am." He moved his hands back.

Missy leaned down and slurped his sac into her mouth, sucking hard enough to make him cry out, then rolling her tongue over and over again on the salty flesh. His balls tightened. He bucked his shaft against her hands. Now it was her turn to smile.

She pulled away, removed her hands and her mouth. He pushed forward, rolling his hips, begging with his body for her to continue. But she had to undo her own pants because she was so fucking wet, so fucking hot that she needed to rub her clit while she was sucking him off or she might just die.

She slipped her fingers into her panties and couldn't help the moan from escaping as she touched her sensitive clit.

Adam moaned too, then did it again when she leaned in and took his cock back into her mouth.

"Missy," he groaned out, "I want to touch you."

But she didn't stop, one hand stroking his dick, sucking him down with her mouth and her fingers working away on her own orgasm. She wasn't about to give him what he wanted, not when she was so fucking close to—

In a flash he had his hands all over her, pulling her off his dick, yanking her up from the chair then spinning her around so that she was bracing her arms against the desk. He had her pants around her ankles in two seconds flat. She was so caught up in her rising orgasm, desperate to keep the friction up so she could follow the cresting pleasure, that it was only a passing realization that he'd somehow busted his restraints again.

She glanced over her shoulder to catch a glimpse of him sheathing his cock in a condom, then lost all coherent thought after that, because he wedged his big, fat dick straight into her pussy.

She couldn't stop herself from crying out as he pounded her hard and fast, drilling into her so that each stroke hit her G-spot and ratcheted her up higher and higher.

"Adam," she moaned. Her body was coiling into the tightest ball, her climax building to impossible heights with every grinding thrust.

And when it crested, she saw stars. He rode her through the pulses of her orgasm, slamming her with even more force, even faster than before until he was bellowing his own release along with her.

He pulled her back, still inside her, his cock pulsing and her pussy quivering. He wrapped one of his big arms around her, caging her close to his body, then put his lips to her throat and kissed her so tenderly that she wanted to melt.

"You're seriously one of the most amazing women I've ever known."

She wanted to believe him. "I've always thought that about you."

"You've thought that I'm a most amazing woman?"

She laughed and tried to swat him. "I've always thought you were amazing, I mean—as a man, as a person." Other words stalled on her tongue. Words like 'love' and 'respect' and a whole lot of wishes for more.

"If you keep this up, I'm going to fall harder than I already have," he murmured against her flesh as he began to kiss her neck.

She wanted to react, her mind suddenly whirling around those words. He was falling for her? She couldn't respond because he latched on to her earlobe, and she lost all coherent thought once again.

Chapter Eleven

He just couldn't get enough of her. There was no way. Even if he rubbed his dick raw from all the fucking, he wouldn't give up a chance to slide into her sweet pussy.

Her body was covered in sweat, a fine sheen that made her pale skin look so silky. Freckles dotted her collarbone and her chest was flush with color. She was in the throes of another mounting orgasm, her eyes half closed, her arms wrapped around his neck.

He was holding her up, pounding her hard against the wall, their clothes half on, half off. The frenzy of fucking her was just so intense that he couldn't even take the time to kick his pants completely off.

He angled her hips so that he could grind harder against her clit and hit just the right pace so that her body arched into him. She started to cry out as her orgasm hit but bit her lip to stop herself, probably so she wouldn't make too much noise. Adam had no idea where her deputy was, but he took her cue, and when his orgasm started to pound through him, he kept his grunts as low key as possible.

Even when his last spurt of cum was spent, he still wanted more. This woman was addictive in all the right ways.

He kissed the line of freckles along her collarbone before pulling away. He could really get used to this kind of life.

He helped her back down to the ground and moved to the side so he could pull the condom off and clean himself up. His mind kept going to the possible ways he could make a long-distance relationship work with Missy. Once this was all over and this shit with Rex and Tommy sorted, Adam wanted to keep Missy in his life, so he had to figure out a way to close the distance between them.

"I'd appreciate it if you kept your illegal investigative activity to yourself. Even better would be if you kept yourself busy in other ways." Missy was buttoning up her shirt, her back to Adam as she said it, feeling more than a little exposed. He'd admitted his feelings earlier…kind of. And she couldn't cope. He was falling for her? What was she supposed to do with that? They didn't even live in the same state, for fuck's sake! "Maybe help your family with the horses instead of playing detective. If you compromise —"

"Hey, I'm not going to compromise anything, Missy. Give me a little credit." He wrapped his arms around her waist and pulled her into his body like he had earlier. This time, though, he was fully clothed. All the same, having his hard body pressed against hers… His arms holding her like they belonged together… She liked it a lot, more than she should. "I've done this before…I mean, not like this exactly" — he kissed her neck, sending shivers through her body once again — "but I've managed to bring down criminals like Elton Morrow — "

Oh shit! She froze. *How in the world does he know about Elton Morrow?* "Why do you think…" She tried for denial, disengaging from his hold so she could turn around and look up at him, but realized in an instant that it wouldn't work. "How did you find out about Elton? Never mind… I don't want to know." She ran her hand through her hair and put some distance between them. *Fuck.* That definitely complicated things. Defeat rolled through her body and she slumped, resting her ass on the edge of her desk. Of course he'd found out about Morrow. "You can't get involved in this. It's too dangerous."

"Missy — "

"No, I'm serious. You need to stop digging now before you trigger something worse happening."

"That's what I'm trying to prevent. Guys like Rex and Elton? They don't need to be treated with a gentle touch. They need to be surveilled, confronted and run out of town."

"You're wrong about that."

"They don't want heat on them, not when so much is at stake. Elton hasn't been caught because he's too slippery."

"Because he has people on the inside, Adam." She sighed. "We need to treat this situation gently."

"Everyone has someone on the inside, including me. Let me call some people."

"No! That's the last thing I want you to do." She put her hand on his arm. "Please just back off and let me do my job. I have things under control."

"You have to look at the evidence my team found." He pulled his phone out. "Rex and his men are being careless with what they talk about. Their guard is down, cocky bastards, and there are plans lying out in the open, detailed maps scattered around their room. I think I know what's going on but—"

"Do *not* turn that phone around. I won't look at your evidence." She put her hand up as if she could physically block him. His insistence was making her feel desperate and angry.

"Missy, this guy is threatening my family, and Tommy is all tangled up it in somehow. I can't back off. Why don't you ease up and work with me? We can get things done quicker together and get rid of this threat."

She dropped her hand. "I can't work with you on this. You're too…" *Tainted by Cowan Enterprises* was the first thing that came into her head, but instead, she said, "Noticeable. I'm surprised the media isn't here already." It was a lame excuse and they both knew it.

"You're just one person, Missy. You've got one deputy…who, I've gotta say, doesn't exactly inspire confidence."

Her temper rose. "I'm capable of—"

"Hey, I'm not saying you're incapable. But you've got to admit that you've got limitations, rules you have to follow. This new commissioner running things seems shady as fuck. I've only just scratched the surface, but I feel like there's more skeletons in that man's closet than even Elton's." Adam lifted his hand to brush some stray hair from her face. "Let me help. I'll make sure you get enough evidence that'll have these assholes running and check your commissioner so he either wises up or steps down."

"No." She folded her arms as she stood, swatting away his hand in the process and bullying him back somehow with her stance. When he cleared a few steps, she moved around to the other side of her desk. *Time to get tough.* "Stop spying on Rex and his men. Stop digging into Commissioner Richardson. *Immediately.* You're a liability to me and also to your family, if I'm going to be honest." She pointed at him. "You take too many risks and you're going to make things worse. You should never have come home."

He flinched as if he'd been struck.

She went for the next obvious target. "What happened between us, the last twenty-four hours" – *just now* – "hasn't meant anything more than a great time, Adam. We haven't suddenly become partners...and we certainly don't have a future." She cleared her throat, feeling the burn of her words all the way to her gut. "Why don't you do what you do best? Wham, bam and you're gone. You're the playboy, right? That's what you're known for in New York. Adam Lancaster, sexiest bodyguard alive. I knew what I was getting into with you. I wasn't expecting anything more, just a few fucks to get it out of our systems. That's all." Not a total lie, but it still felt like shit to say the words. Even if that was where she'd started, somewhere along the way, it wasn't where she'd ended up.

She had to get him off this case. Now that he'd found out about Elton, it was only a matter of time before he figured out the extent of the commissioner's involvement, and that was a can of worms she couldn't let him open.

"Oh yeah? That's all it was? I'm just a walking cock, ready to serve your needs and nothing more?" Adam narrowed his eyes. "You don't know a thing about me...never have."

"I can say the same right back at you. Once upon a time you told me that I was a nobody, a dirty girl that no man would find attractive. An ugly duckling." She was revisiting this without much thought. It just started spilling out of her mouth, like she was still hurt from the words, like the revenge she'd gotten all those years ago hadn't actually repaired anything for her. There was something deeply psychological going on here, but she didn't have the time or energy to reflect on it.

He opened his mouth. She raised a hand.

"You probably don't remember, but I do. Guys like you never remember shitty things like that." Her heart was hammering so hard that she felt it in her throat. "It was the summer that you left. You were out by the river, sulking or something, and I stumbled upon you." Okay, she had totally been stalking him at that age. "I asked you what was up, and you snapped at me for ruining the quiet. Remember?" She didn't wait for him to respond, but she could tell by his eyes that he maybe did remember—or he was starting to, anyway. "I figured you were sulking over a girl or something, so I made an off-handed comment about it and wham. You hit me with your version of tough love. You said—"

"That no guy was ever going to want to hang out with a girl like you, not unless you cleaned yourself up. *'Ever consider a hairbrush, Missy?'*" he finished. "*'You don't have to go around looking so run-down all the time. You're like the ugly little duckling in that story, except no one can see your potential under all the dirt.'*"

Missy's throat tightened. He'd embarrassed her, made her feel like her worth was all tied up in her appearance.

"Missy, I'm so—"

"Yeah, sure, *now* you are," she cut him off. "That night five years ago? That was about revenge, pure and simple." Was she saying this out loud to make it real? "Proving to myself that a guy like you—a playboy, Mr. Sexy—yeah, I could entice you. I'm not the same girl I was—the gangly, annoying little teenager who followed you around everywhere…the girl you crushed with a few careless comments. I proved that someone like you could fall for someone like me. Last night, this morning, I proved it again. What happened between us meant nothing more than that. I scratched an itch and now I'm satisfied." The half-truths tasted bitter to her, like she was getting things off her chest but at the same time choking on the poison of what she was uttering out loud.

His eyes shuttered and she felt like a wall was forming between them once again. *Good. Better that way.*

She needed him gone, for his own safety and for her sanity. He'd already found out too much and she'd given too much. Adam was never going to be a good choice for her, no matter how badly she wanted it.

"You mean that?" His voice cracked and it nearly broke her resolve. "All this has been about payback and nothing more? All you want from me is a few fucks and that's it?"

She straightened her back, hardened her eyes and fought with everything in her power not to suck it all back and beg him to forgive her. "Yes. What else would I want from someone like you?"

Despite her harsh words, her heart was hurting. The look on his face was enough to make her regret what she'd said, those blue eyes so sad all of a sudden. *Fuck, what have I done?*

He didn't say another word. He just nodded once then turned and left. He didn't even slam the door behind him.

No anger. No argument. Just closure. That was what she'd wanted, right?

No! She wanted to stop him, to chase after him. "Don't." She whispered to herself and planted her feet firmly so she wouldn't take a step toward the door. All the same, tears burned her eyes. She needed him to leave. It was for his own good, she repeated to herself. So why was it feeling like her heart was crushing in on itself? Like she was letting someone go who she needed by her side?

A car door slammed and an engine roared to life, then the crunching of gravel as Adam's SUV presumably drove away.

She sucked in a deep breath, then let it all out. Every emotion she'd kept bottled for those few moments when she'd uttered such hateful lies came out in a rush. Yeah, she'd thought she'd done it for revenge that night five years ago, to get back at Adam for his cruel words, but sometime in the last twenty-four hours she realized that she'd actually done it because she wanted him more than any other man she'd ever met. She'd been attracted to Adam from the time that she had been a gangly teen, probably before that too, and she wanted him now, as a full-blown adult. He'd said he was falling for her and she couldn't let that happen, not when she was falling for him too.

Her heart wanted him. And that was some seriously fucked up shit, because she knew that in no possible way would their lives ever fit together. She'd never get Adam the way she wanted him, all to herself, not with the life he was used to living. So, better to cut ties and start the process of getting over him...again.

Last night and this morning had been a mistake, if only because it was going to make it harder for her to stay away.

She knew enough about him to know that Adam was going to put himself in danger to save his family too. She couldn't take her time with this. Things were getting too hot now that Adam was involved. She'd already had a call from Commissioner Richardson's assistant, asking questions about Adam and his involvement with things. She'd been warned, in so many words, that she needed to keep Adam the hell away from Rex and his men. The 'or else' had been implied.

Commissioner Edward Richardson was not from Grimshield. He didn't know Adam or the Lancasters. He didn't know her very well, either. And he didn't spend a lot of time in town, not when his office was in Hockly, the next town over. But he did have a strong philosophy on cutting the fat, as he liked to say, from the budgets, and his assistant had made it clear that more funding cuts would be coming her way if she didn't follow orders—funding cuts that would make her job disappear.

As much as she liked to follow the rules, in this case she knew she couldn't. She was the sheriff of Grimshield, and she had an obligation to get to the bottom of things. Rex and his men were not good for her town, and it was her job to keep everyone safe.

She had to get into Rex's rooms to see those maps Adam had mentioned, decide if they would give her what she needed then figure out how to make the information viable for her investigation. Time was running out. She could feel it.

She picked up the phone. "Lacey...hey, remember what we talked about the other day? I need that to happen today, like...right now."

Chapter Twelve

Adam was in a shit mood for the rest of the morning after leaving Missy and her harsh words behind. He hadn't been expecting a fucking marriage proposal or anything, but after the last twenty-four hours they'd had, he'd at least expected a little warmth. Was that too much to ask?

Apparently, yes.

She'd been cold and dismissive, and he felt...well, insulted and hurt actually. Probably just as dismissed and in pain as she had felt way back on that day so long ago that he'd hurt her so badly—when he'd been so caught up in himself and his own problems that he'd discounted her and had obviously damaged her feelings beyond repair, and probably embarrassed the hell out of her too.

Fuck. He was sorry. He wished she would listen to him about that. And he understood her need for revenge. He didn't actually mind her version of revenge, but this shit that came after—not giving him a chance to speak, to talk to it out? Yeah, that was totally not cool.

He hadn't lied when he'd said he was falling for her. He realized, though, that words like that probably freaked Missy the hell out. The last thing she'd want was baggage with him. He should have kept his mouth closed and enjoyed the time he had with her. Then maybe after a while, she'd have come around. Instead, he'd pushed her away with his hastily blurted truth.

And now he was once again dwelling on the fact that no one seemed to want him around except for his mom, and that he'd been an asshole to Missy fifteen years ago in the same way as Missy had been to him today — and it felt like shit.

Lacey was just getting off the phone when Adam walked into the pub. He knew he was taking a calculated risk in even entering the hotel, but he had things to accomplish and his plans started at Lacey's

"Well, if it isn't Adam Lancaster in the flesh! Boy, come here and give me a hug! I need to feel if all those muscles are real." Lacey Peters was the feistiest elderly woman Adam had ever known, and she'd seemed elderly for the entire time Adam had known her, basically his whole life. Her wrinkles had been deeply rooted for decades, it seemed. Her age, however, had never slowed her down much. She might be old as dirt, but she was full of fire and moved like she wasn't a day older than thirty.

She came around the bar and wrapped Adam in a hug that filled him with so much warmth that his bad mood just slipped away. Her hugs were magical like that. And that was why he was really here.

"You've grown up, haven't you?" She gave him a tight squeeze before pulling back a bit to get a look at him. "I'm so glad you're here!" Her smile was infectious, and Adam couldn't help but smile back.

"You haven't changed one bit, Ms. Lacey, just as beautiful as ever."

She patted her hair and fluttered her eyelashes. "Oh, you do flatter, don't you, boy?" She motioned to the bar. "It's a little early for a drink, but I could get you something to eat. Kev's in the kitchen getting lunch ready for our guests." She rolled her eyes. "A buffet is preferred by some of the men staying here, so we've just started doing it every day now."

"Wish I could, but I've got to get back to the ranch." Adam glanced toward the main staircase that was on the other side of the room. There was no sign of Rex and his men, but that didn't mean they weren't around. "I'm only here to check in, maybe get a key to my room."

"Oh, yes, of course." Lacey moved toward the small office on the other side of the bar. "I held the room for ya, just like ya asked." She frowned over her shoulder. "You're not planning on staying here tonight, are ya?"

"Not right now, no, but there may be a time that I do, so I'd like to be able to access my room."

"Of course, of course." She waved him off. "I'll just be a minute."

She left the room and he got to work quickly placing his bugs. He'd talked to Lacey about this briefly on the phone, just letting her know that he'd be investigating Rex's men, but he'd told her that he didn't want her to know exactly how, because he didn't want her to be held liable for any invasion of privacy if he got caught doing it. She was fine with whatever he had planned. She'd let him know that she was sick as hell of the way Rex and his men were treating people in town, including her, and she was ready for them to leave. She also let Adam know that Rex and the men sat around and boasted about a lot of things she wished someone else could hear when they were eating and drinking in the pub. That was when Adam had known what he had to do.

They'd devised a plan for her to leave the room so he could get things set up and hopefully take care of her problem in a few days.

She was gone for more than ten minutes. That was plenty of time for him to bug the room.

"So sorry that took so long, Adam, but I just needed to take a call and sort some plans out." She winked at him as she handed over his room key. "I've got you at the end of the hall in room five."

"Thanks, Ms. Lacey. I appreciate it." They shared a meaningful look and he nodded to let her know that the job was complete.

"Well, lunch will be ready shortly. You're sure you can't stay? It's included in the price of the room."

"No, ma'am, I've got to get back. Mom's probably cooking up a bunch of food too."

"Well, I'd say she likely is, with the size of you!" Lacey winked again then patted him on the arm. "Big, strong boy like you needs nourishment. You make sure to come here for one meal at least before you head home. I'd like to feed ya, too."

Adam grinned. "I will for sure. And thanks again for holding the room. Never do know when things will get too close for comfort back home."

"Oh, yes, yes, I understand that all too well. Sensible plan having an option available. Keeps the tempers from getting the best of ya." She squeezed his arm, letting him know that she remembered the old tensions that had existed between him and his dad all those years ago.

He left with a smile on his face. Lacey had always been the kindest lady and had also been the person who knew what was going on with everyone. She'd given him warm milk and cookies on more than one occasion when he'd run away from home after a fight with his dad, and had always managed to get him smiling again so he'd go back. The least he could do was pay for a room, even if he probably wasn't going to use it.

His phone was buzzing by the time he made it back to his rental. "Hey, boss, you missin' me?" Adam turned the engine on then transferred the call to hands free.

"Of course I miss you, Adam. We all do." Sabine's voice was all business, as usual, but he could tell that she was smiling because, in truth, they were good friends and loved each other. "How are things going back home?"

"As expected." *Mostly.* He'd tell her about Missy once he was back in New York. They'd been through enough shit in their time together that secrets weren't really a thing between them. She was his boss, sure, but he trusted her with his life. She knew all about his family situation as well, so she'd already know that 'as expected' meant his dad was being his usual pissy self. "I talked to Bret this morning. He filled me in on the attempted hack on our system. I'm pretty sure it's linked to things going down here." Adam suspected this was Rex's doing, maybe at the request of Elton Morrow, or maybe it was some dirty work ordered by the commissioner. Either way, Adam had definitely caught someone's attention and they'd attempted to hack into Cowan Enterprises' systems.

"Yes, he updated me first thing. I wasn't worried. I knew you had it under control." She paused for a second to give one of her assistants some direction, then came back on the line. "When do you think you'll have this wrapped up? Or better yet, what can I do to help you get this wrapped up so that you're back here with me?" She was probably worried about the toll being back home would have on Adam. She'd said as much when he'd told her he needed to help his mother in Grimshield. With the history he had with his dad, too much time spent there would bring back old wounds that she likely didn't want him suffering.

"I've got a few leads going now, just waiting for some pay-dirt. Found out that Elton Morrow is involved."

Sabine sucked in a deep breath. "Well, that's all kinds of fucked up, then." She knew just as well as Adam did that Elton Morrow was supplying most of the northern states' elite with their recreational drugs. He'd been a primary source for Sabine, back in the day. "He's a dangerous man."

"I know, and don't worry. I'm not taking any risks."

"Adam…"

"I'm not taking too many risks." He laughed. "But seriously, I've got it under control. I'm just trying to nail down what the angle is here. It doesn't make sense that they want my folks' ranch. They're saying Tommy owes some huge debt and they need some kind of collateral, but when Tommy first came home, he was trying to convince Mom and Dad to sell the place. So, there's two different stories going on and I need to figure out what the truth of it all is."

"Yeah, that doesn't make sense." She was typing on her computer. He could hear the clickety-clack of her nails on the keys. "They want your parents out of there for some reason. Tommy maybe tried to approach it as an asset, but the guys who are really calling the shots are approaching it differently. Probably figured they could scare your parents off the land, not realizing you were part of the family."

Adam snorted. "If Dad could have his way, I wouldn't be."

"Well, he's a dickhead." Never one to mince words, Sabine always was blunt about her feelings for Adam's father. "As you know, Elton Morrow is a slippery man, and everything he does is to enhance distribution lines. If he wants your parents' ranch that badly, then there's got to be something you're not seeing and it's got to be connected to his business."

"We're not on a major highway. We're not a port for ships or even a stop for trains. But you're right. There's something more going on here."

Adam needed to get his hands on those maps and figure out what the fuck was going on, because he was sure they were at the heart of this mystery.

"I can call in some favors if needed. Get you some backup."

Adam turned onto the ranch's long driveway. "I appreciate that, Sabine, but leave it with me for now." Sabine knew a lot of important people—important, powerful people. He didn't want things to get crazy just yet. Missy was investigating in her way, Adam in his, but there was something they were both missing— or at least something Adam wasn't quite seeing.

Sabine stopped typing. "Just say the word."

"Thanks. I'll keep you posted." He pulled up to the house. His mother was hanging laundry in the yard. She had a pile of it lying in a basket at her feet. By the looks of it all, Adam knew it would take her over an hour to get it up on the lines. "I've got to go, but I'll give you a call tomorrow."

"Take care, Adam. We want you home in one piece." She'd probably meant psychologically. She knew how damaging families could be.

"No worries, boss. Nothing going on here that will fuck with my head or my heart." *Except, possibly, for a certain sheriff.* "We'll talk soon."

He ended the call then got out of the SUV. "Hey, Mom, you need a hand with that?"

* * * *

Later that day, Adam was back in his loft, checking the feeds from Rex's guys' various computers and phones and thinking about Missy again.

He wasn't obsessed with her. *Okay, maybe I'm a little bit obsessed with her.* She clearly had some anger issues directly connected to him and things he'd said to her years ago, but it was also obvious that she was totally into him, if only maybe for his body. She didn't like who he was—or who she thought he was—and he wondered if there was a way to change that. The truth of the matter was that he was really into Missy, and not just because of her smokin' hot body. She was a fierce person and cared deeply for the people she considered under her protection, which amounted to everyone in Grimshield. She was determined too, and yes, stubborn, but he could work with that. He really was falling for her, falling hard, and he wanted to see what the future might hold for them.

But he needed her to lower her defenses and give him a chance. She needed to trust him.

He clicked over to another screen that would show him the four rooms at Lacey's where Rex's men were staying. All four cameras were active, which meant that the men had their computers on. Adam could activate the cameras, even if the computers were dormant, as long as the lids were up, but that would make the little light on their screens flare to life. It was easier and less risky to use the cameras when the computers were being used. He could see a good portion of each room. One of the men was coming out of the bathroom, one was reading something on the bed, another was lying down and the fourth was talking on his phone. Adam had access to that particular phone.

Adam switched over to the audio program and isolated that guy's conversation.

"Are you sure this is necessary?" he said.

"The old bag says we have to vacate for at least two hours so the inspector can check all the rooms and do some kind of spraying, so yeah, it seems necessary. We can get a few things done that need doing." Adam recognized Rex's voice.

"Got it."

"Grab the guys and I'll meet you downstairs. We'll take one truck."

Adam watched as the guy he was listening to ended the call and left the room. A few seconds later, there was a knock on another door, and one by one, each of the Cooper men left. Adam would have about ten minutes, give or take, before the screens would go black. With the men gone from the rooms, he had no one to spy on, so it didn't really matter.

He leaned back and stared at the screens. Lacey hadn't mentioned anything about an exterminator coming by. He switched over to the audio feed from the bugs he'd planted in the pub. Lacey's voice flooded his speakers.

"No one can be in the building while the exterminator is here, so thank you, Mr. Cooper, for agreeing to leave for the time being. I'm sorry for the inconvenience."

"I expect compensation," Rex grumbled.

"Of course. As I said, dinner is on me at Quincey's. I believe they've opened one of their famous vintage reds for you. You'll have a wonderful meal." The sound of the front door opening then closing echoed through the speakers.

There was a minute of silence, no more, then the door opened again.

"Ah, Carl, thanks for coming. You want a coffee?"

"Hey, Lacey, sure thing. Been a long day." There was some grunting that Adam took to be Carl the exterminator taking a seat at the bar. "So what's this about some cockroaches in the kitchen?"

Adam grimaced.

"Oh, right, yeah, I think I was just seeing things." Lacey laughed.

"Well, I'll take a look around when I'm done."

"I appreciate that, Carl. Pie?"

Adam frowned. Something about this sounded very strange. Was Lacey running some kind of scheme to get Rex and his men out of the building?

Movement caught the corner of his eye and he flicked his gaze to the split screens on his computer. The door of one of the men's rooms upstairs slowly opened. *What the…?* Adam leaned forward, squinting at the screen.

Missy slipped into the room looking like she was totally doing something that pushed the boundaries of legal territory. "Well now, this is an interesting development, Sheriff." Adam folded his arms and leaned back, smirking as he watched Miss High-and-Mighty-Righteous-Law-Abider compromise her own investigation by breaking and entering one of Rex's rented rooms.

Chapter Thirteen

Missy knew she had at least an hour — an hour to break the law — which was so ironic considering the grief she'd given Adam over this very sketchy form of investigating. But she needed to speed this along because she knew time was running out. She had to be the one who figured out what Rex was up to, to find the link between the commissioner and Elton Morrow. It was the only way to keep Adam safe, she was sure. At least that was what her gut was telling her.

So, she and Lacey had devised this plan to get Rex and his men out of the building for a while, allowing her access to the rooms. It wasn't like she was breaking and entering. Lacey had given her a master key.

Right, keep telling yourself that, sister.

She was only searching for the right direction. She wasn't going to use anything she found to directly implicate Rex and his men. But she did need to know what Adam had found. He'd said there were maps, and she needed to see them.

She sighed to herself. This was wrong, she knew, but her motivation was right and she was keeping Adam safe by not letting him become directly involved.

It wasn't just what Adam had said about the maps that had Missy wanting to search the rooms, though. Lacey had told her about the papers constantly strewn all around when she went into clean. The men didn't actually want her in their rooms, but she made a point to enter unexpectedly at least once every few days. They'd signed a contract, she'd said, so they'd already given her permission to enter whenever she'd wanted. And Lacey knew that the documents were important, even if she couldn't actually see what they were, because every time she invaded their space, they all scrambled to cover the papers up or shift everything so she wouldn't be able to read them. That was what Lacey had told Missy long before Adam had shown up in town.

She'd been waiting for the right opportunity to get a search warrant. Of course, that was wishful thinking, because Rex had ways around a warrant ever being issued, ways that Missy suspected involved bribing some key people like the commissioner. She'd tried several times and had learned every time, just how slippery Rex was.

She did a quick scan of the room. It was one of the larger suites with a bathroom attached and a couch along one wall. There were two double beds and Lacey had told her that this was Rex's room, which he shared with one of the other men. There was a table in the far corner and yes, it was covered with papers. *One would think that for a group of guys trying to conduct shady business, they'd be a little more careful.* Missy beelined for the table as a good place to start.

So far, her investigation had yielded some information. The law enforcement buddies who'd given her the heads-up had told her about the properties Rex had acquired in the neighboring counties. He'd allegedly taken them by coercion of some sort. Homeowners who hadn't previously wanted to sell were suddenly moving out fast, usually with a fat pocket full of hush money. But then the property would sit empty, acres and acres of prime land with no activity except for the occasional security check here and there. It was baffling to all involved.

Because Rex was connected to Elton Morrow, everyone she'd talked to had suspicions this was somehow linked to drug trafficking, but of course there was never any proof, despite their best efforts. The common denominator, other than Rex and his men, was the commissioner — or rather, the commissioner's real estate brother, Neil Richardson. Every single property the men had acquired so far had been brokered by Neil.

When Adam had mentioned the maps, Missy knew she had to see them. The maps might tell her more about the plan that had Rex buying up property on behalf of his boss, Elton. If Rex wanted the Lancaster ranch, there had to be a reason, one that no one else was seeing.

So she was rifling around, looking through the papers, which all seemed to be property tax bills from various locations but again, with no discernible pattern. Why would Elton want those particular properties? And why the Lancaster ranch? Sure, it was a nice piece of land, but to then let it sit idle like all the other properties he had acquired? Yeah, that was super sketchy.

Her instinct was to pile the papers up neatly, but she had to stop herself from doing that. Tidying up would tip Rex off that someone had been there. It physically pained her to toss the papers aside after looking at them, but she just had to accept that this wasn't her mess.

She'd been searching for no more than ten minutes when she heard a creak outside the door and froze. Had she heard that or was her imagination getting the better of her? She pulled her phone out to check for a text from Lacey, who would warn her if the men returned. Nothing.

There was another creak. Someone was definitely outside the door.

Fuck!

Missy scanned the room. *The closet.* Not the best hiding spot but good in a pinch. She started toward it then froze again, because there was a knock on the door.

"Missy," a voice hissed. "It's Adam. Let me in."

Adam? Without thinking too hard on it, she opened the door. "What are you doing here?"

He didn't answer. Instead, he pushed into the room.

"You can't be in here. You're ruin—"

"You can't be in here either." He grunted as he lifted the mattress and nodded downward. "Grab those, would ya?"

Missy had an argument on the tip of her tongue but swallowed it when she saw the maps lying between the mattresses. "How'd you know—? Never mind." She'd forgotten about his spyware. *Stupid oversight.* Of course he'd seen every move she'd just made, because he had access to the computers in the room. There was one on the table and...yep...one on the nightstand—both opened, both windows into this room as far as Adam and his illegal activities were concerned.

She pulled the maps out carefully so that they didn't rip then put them on the table as Adam lowered the mattress. She tried not to stare at how effortless that all seemed to him or how his muscles flexed and budged. She definitely didn't look at his ass as he was squatting to drop the mattress soundlessly.

As he straightened, she focused her attention to the maps. "These are of Grimshield and the counties surrounding it. Surveyors' maps…" She flipped to the next one, which was marked up. "There's your folks' place." Which was also marked, the property line outlined in red.

Adam was standing next to her at this point, his eyes narrowed as he scanned the map. He slid the next one out and laid it side by side with the one Missy had. "Notice anything?"

She noticed how close Adam was standing to her. She noticed how he smelled, which was deliciously tempting. She noticed the heat he gave off and how his arm swayed closer to her. *Focus!* Missy looked at the lines marking the Lancaster property. "The Shield River," she blurted, then traced her finger along the twisty path of the winding river as it trailed from one map to the next. "It goes through your back property." Which she knew first-hand because she'd swum there as a kid many times.

"And it goes all the way to the Missouri."

"Holy shit, yes it does!" They looked up at each other.

"Would be a discreet way of trafficking product to the north, wouldn't you say? The Missouri comes pretty close to Canada."

"Those rivers aren't patrolled much. The hunting and gaming officers have huge swaths of land to cover and they're looking for illegal fishing and hunting, not boats potentially carrying drugs up river," Missy said as she trailed the river with her finger. "At least not around here, anyway."

"Exactly." Adam shifted the map aside and got out his phone.

"What are you doing?"

"Taking pictures." The 'duh' was implied.

"You can't do that! We won't be able to use —"

"No, *you* won't be able to use the information. Not officially anyway." He snapped a few pictures at different angles then shifted the map so he could get a clearer view of the next one.

"But you can?" She touched his arm and he paused what he was doing to look at her. Her heart skipped a beat. He was just so damn... She couldn't finish that thought, no matter how much she wanted to. *Clean break. No more sex.* She needed to keep a distance. "What do you have planned? Tell me, Adam."

"Nothing for you to worry about." He smirked. "You don't want to know, remember?"

"Adam —" Her phone buzzed, two quick messages that told her their time had run out. She pulled it out and glanced at the screen. "It's from Lacey."

Stalling. You have two minutes.

"Shit, they're back! We need to get out of here."

"Fuck! I thought Lacey said the exterminator would be busy for a while still." Adam pulled the maps off the table and handed them to Missy. "Aren't they supposed to be eating at Quincey's?"

She was about to ask how he knew that but realized that he had his ways and he was right. She didn't want to know.

"Something must have gone wrong." Rex wasn't stupid. He'd thwarted her various attempts to catch him in the act of threatening the Lancasters too. It was like he knew what she was going to do before she even did it. Maybe he had bugged her office...or used some kind of spyware like Adam had used and was tracking her moves.

Adam lifted the mattress and Missy slid the maps back in between.

"Careful... They need to go in exactly like we found them."

Missy adjusted the maps so they lay flat. She wasn't sure what direction they had been facing when she'd pulled them out, other than picture-side up, so she hoped she'd gotten the direction right. She wasn't sure if Rex would notice if they were upside-down, but she wouldn't put it past him. "Done."

With a huff, Adam lowered the mattress. "Let's go."

Adam listened at the door for a few seconds before slowly opening it and peering both ways in the hall. "We're good." He grabbed her hand.

Her heart was frantically racing but she didn't pull away.

If they got caught, her entire investigation would be blown. Rex would raise a ruckus for sure and she'd lose her job. What on earth had she been thinking, going into his room like this? She wasn't reckless. Everything she did was calculated. Planned. Law-abiding.

Adam tugged her hand, his fingers entwined with hers.

They made it to the top of the stairs, but the voices of Rex and his men filtered up close enough to tell them that the men were just at the bottom.

"We can't go that way," Adam whispered. He pointed to the end of the hall where there was a large window. "Fire escape."

Missy nodded. They moved quickly, but just as they got to the window, they both heard Rex's voice getting closer. He was coming up the stairs.

"Fuck, fuck, fuck!" Missy whispered. They'd never make it out in time.

Adam yanked her backward.

"What are you—"

He slipped a key into a lock, turned it, then opened the door. He quickly shoved her inside, following closely behind.

She was leaning into him, inhaling him, too close…much too close. He shut the door softly then leaned closer. She leaned closer too. He was listening, his ear pressed against the door.

Missy's phone buzzed. She looked down at the message.

Rex is upstairs with one of them. Three others are down here drinking. You two need to stay put for now. He's suspicious.

"Fuck," Missy muttered.

Adam glanced over at her, an eyebrow cocked.

"We're stuck here for a while," she said, turning her phone so he could read for himself.

"So it seems." His face broke into a sly grin. "That gives us some time for your punishment."

Chapter Fourteen

"Punishment! For what?"

He turned fully toward her, his big body dwarfing hers. "For lying to me, for starters." The grin was gone and in its place was a look of pure dominance.

Missy shivered as a rush of lust ran through her. "I didn't lie—"

"Yes, you did." He wasn't touching her, but his penetrating gaze alone had her body revving up.

Her nipples hardened. Her pussy clenched. *This is so inappropriate.* What was with this man that he had her amped up at all the wrong times?

"You told me that I'd be compromising the investigation with my tactics, and yet here we are." He waved one hand around.

"I had to see—"

"And you lied about not wanting me around." He leaned into her then, forcing her back until she was against the wall. "You lied about scratching an itch."

"No, I, I..." she moaned, all words lost when he nuzzled her throat, sucking her skin in a wholly sensual way.

Flame to accelerant. Just like that, her body was on fire.

She couldn't deny this man — not now, not ever. And a part of her wanted to be punished. She had lied. She had been a hypocrite, and worse, she'd compromised her own investigation.

He gripped her ass and lifted her so she could wrap her legs around his body. *Fuck keeping a distance.* She wanted him and he wanted her and they were alone with time to kill. Maybe if she kept scratching that itch, she'd actually get him out of her system.

Yeah, right.

He moved her to the bed and set her down. When he pulled away and straightened up, his expression was all business. "Take your clothes off, right down to your bra and panties. Leave those on." He spoke quietly but sternly, making her want to snap back at him. But the look on his face said backtalk wouldn't go over well. There was something so irresistible about Adam right now — more than usual, if that were possible.

He stood back, his arms crossed, and watched her undress. Her hands were shaking, but not because she was scared. No, this was all excitement. She undid her utility belt and set it aside then started to unbutton her shirt, his eyes on her making her heart pound harder and her body quiver. He looked so imposing, so in charge.

"We don't have all day. Move it or you'll get a handprint on your ass."

Missy paused, her eyes went wide, and she did let out a snort. "I doubt that'll happen."

In a flash Adam was on her, pulling her over his knee like she was a misbehaving child. It was shocking how strong he was, moving her like she weighed nothing as he flopped down on the bed and trapped her on his lap so that she couldn't move beyond some squirming.

Before she had a chance to think too hard on it, he hit her ass with his palm. Hard. She jolted and started to cry out, but he clamped his hand over her mouth and shushed her. "Quiet."

She struggled to get away but he held her tight and did it again.

"You wanna be a smart mouth? Maybe we'll get your mouth working on something big enough to shut you up." He pushed her down so that her knees hit the floor. "Unzip my pants."

Her ass was burning. She had no doubt that her cheeks were red. Maybe there was even a handprint like he'd promised.

She did as she was told. And when she unzipped his pants, his dick sprang out. He wasn't wearing underwear, as usual. Her mouth was watering.

Fuck, she loved his cock.

"Kiss it."

She leaned forward and gently kissed the tip of his dick.

"Open your mouth and suck me off. Go deep, Missy, as far as you can."

She leaned closer, opened her mouth and —

"Look at me when you do it."

She snapped her eyes up to meet his then slipped his cock past her lips. He filled her up, stretched her mouth, and she knew she wouldn't be able to take him all down. But she did as she had been told and worked him as far back as she could without gagging.

He nudged her, lifting his hips slightly so that she could feel the tip of his dick against the back of her throat.

He reached forward and rubbed his hand over her tit, squeezing her through her bra. Their eyes were still locked as Missy slowly pulled herself up, pressing her tongue against his shaft until her lips were curled around the tip.

He moaned and his eyes fluttered, so she slid back down again, coating him with her saliva, making his flesh slick as his cock pulsed for her. She could taste his pre-cum. The salty tang was familiar now. She wanted him to come down her throat, so she worked him as best she could and lifted her hand so she could cup his balls at the same time.

His eyes said he liked that very much.

"You're good at sucking cock, Missy. I like seeing you on your knees too."

And she liked his praise, so she sucked and licked and stroked harder, faster, gently kneading his balls at the same time.

His hand was still on her tit, teasing her through the fabric of her bra. She wanted skin-to-skin contact. She wanted everything all at the same time.

Patience, Missy. You'll get there.

He let her suck him off for another few minutes, watching her the entire time. His eyes on her were making her even more wet than she already was. She wanted to please him, to pleasure him.

"That's enough," he grunted, his voice still quiet but firm. "Get back on the bed and take your pants off. No comments or I'll punish you again."

She almost wanted to be punished. But she did as she was told, stripping down to her panties as she got back on the bed.

He was searching the room for something…curtain ties, apparently. When he came back to the bed, he motioned for her to back up. "Payback's a bitch." He grinned wickedly. "Put your wrists together."

She felt a shiver of excitement and did what she was told. Adam in control was very stimulating, maybe more so than when she took control. She held her wrists out to him. He kicked his pants off and climbed onto the bed with her. His dick was bobbing in front of him, and he grabbed her arms and yanked her forward.

"Hold them close. I'm going to tie this tight, but not so tight that you lose circulation, okay?"

She nodded then watched with fascination as he wrapped the curtain tie around her wrists in such a way that it crisscrossed before he yanked it tightly, making her wrists feel bonded together. He tied the two ends then lifted her arms.

"Lie back," he ordered. And he climbed up her body as she slid down, lifting her arms over her head and back until she was almost touching the headboard. His dick was in her face, right at her lips, and she wanted to taste him again. "Do *not* put your lips on my dick."

Missy glanced up to see him staring down at her with a stern look on his face. *How does he know what I'm thinking?*

He shook his head then refocused on what he was doing. He looped the other curtain tie between her arms then hoisted her partly up as he tied the other ends to the headboard. He then shoved the pillows under her back so she wasn't suspended without support. She could find a way to escape if she wanted it. He'd left one of the ends dangling between her fingers so all she'd have to do was tug and she'd be free. It was very considerate of him, and it eased the minute feeling of anxiety she'd had at the idea of being trapped. She didn't mind being at Adam's mercy right now, but it was good knowing she could untie herself if she needed to.

His dick was still there, inches away from her lips. She could just lean forward a bit and—

"You touch my dick right now and I'm going to spank your bare ass."

She stuck her tongue out and came so close to tasting him again.

He laughed, shook his head, then moved down her body. "You don't do well with orders, do you?"

"I like to be in charge."

"Yeah, I noticed." He ran his finger lightly over the edge of her panties and across her stomach. He was sitting on her legs, trapping them without putting his full weight down. "I'm in charge now. I'm going to tell you when you can come, and if you obey me, I'll give you a big reward."

Obey him? She was about to scoff when he yanked her panties up so that they slipped between her lips and abraded her already sensitive clit. She gasped and tried to roll her hips but he was still on her legs, so she couldn't move beyond a little wiggle.

"I like your sweet pussy." He licked his lips.

Missy's cheeks ignited all over again.

He reached behind her back and unlatched her bra, then brought his hands around so that he could cup her breasts.

"You have the most perfect tits, Missy. Seriously, I could suck them all day."

She wanted to squirm, to cover her face...all this sexy talk was making her feel like she could burn up with embarrassment. But she loved it too. She wanted more.

He brushed his thumbs over her nipples then leaned down and licked one, then the other. "They look like ripe little buds." He flicked both before rolling them between his fingers and thumbs.

She bucked her hips. *Ah, yes...* She liked having her nipples played with so much.

"Hmmm, I think you like that, don't you?" He leaned down again and pulled her nipple into his mouth, swirling it with his tongue while he flicked and pinched her other one with his fingers.

The dual sensation of having her breasts played with while the weight of him on her lower body increased was so fucking hot she wanted to explode, and she couldn't help the little moans that slipped out of her mouth.

He flicked his eyes up, his lips and fingers still working away, and she locked in on him. They were so blue. She could get lost in how blue they were. She'd always loved his eyes. There was so much expression there, and right now, she realized that they were sparkling with mischief.

He pulled back, letting her nipple slip from his mouth.

"I'm going to suck your pussy, baby...but remember... You don't get to come until I say you get to come. Understand?"

Missy gulped then nodded. She wasn't sure how she could stop herself from coming when everything Adam did made her feel so damn amazing.

"Good girl."

He shifted down so that he was straddling her shins, then parted her legs so that her knees were bent and her pussy was on display. She still had her panties on and they were still wedged up tight. He yanked on them again, torqueing the fabric against her clit, then ran his finger along one side of her pussy. She jolted.

He grinned.

Then he moved off the bed completely and pulled her panties from her body. "No need for these." And when he came back, he spread her legs wider and she couldn't feel more exposed.

"Your pussy is glistening. It looks like dessert, and I want to eat it up."

She shivered as he gazed at her, feeling so vulnerable and so sexy at the same time. He ran his fingers along the sides of her pussy before spreading her lips then leaning in and licking her from bottom to top. The jolt of his tongue on her made her buck, and he laid his hand down on her hip and kept her in place.

His mouth on her pussy was pure magic.

He licked and sucked at her clit then ran his tongue up and down and inside her, groaning the whole time as though he was eating the most delicious dessert of his life. She was writhing and pulsing, her whole body on fire for this man. She wanted to touch herself, to play with her nipples, but every time she tried, she felt the tug of the bonds that held her wrists and moaned in frustration.

Adam just kept licking until she was so amped up, so ripe for release that she kind of forgot about his little permission thing. Her orgasm crested so quickly that she was coming before she had a chance to really think about it.

He growled through her climax, and when she was done shuddering and shaking, he looked up at her and grinned in the most devilish way. "Oh, baby, you're going to pay for that."

He moved up her body, which was super-sensitive now that she'd come, and left a trail of tender kisses until he got to her nipples. He latched on and she jolted again, arching up with the intensity of his mouth on her flesh.

He rolled his finger over her clit and she just about tore her wrists out of the bindings—or tried to, anyway. "What are you doing?"

"Oh, I'm going to make you come again...and again..."

She was going to lose her mind. "I thought you didn't want me to come," she gasped.

"Oh, I want you to come...when I tell you to." He flashed that grin at her again then reached up and unlatched her wrists from the headboard. "Flip over."

He kept her wrists tied together but didn't reattach her to the bed. Instead he positioned her just right, her ass up high, and before she knew what was going on, she felt the sting of his hand on her bare ass.

She stifled a yelp, biting down on her bottom lip. Her skin was on fire in an instant. She could feel the imprint of his palm. She shifted forward, trying to move away from the next spank, but it didn't come. Instead, he slipped his fingers inside her pussy, using his thumb to circle her clit so she was rocking backward.

He smacked her again, sending her forward, making her moan, then rocked her clit and pumped her pussy again. And so it went—smack, rub, stroke, smack—until she was a writhing, moaning mess. Ready to come again, she was so revved up that she was sure the next spank would send her overboard.

"No coming, Missy," he commanded.

But she didn't know how to hold back. "Adam, it's too…oh my…I'm going to—"

He smacked her ass. She felt the burn right down to her core and her pussy started to spasm so hard that she saw stars.

He cursed, then before her orgasm was over, he was inside her, drilling her so hard that her head nearly hit the headboard. She rocked forward and back, her tits swaying as his cock filled her and made her climax roll out longer, more intensely. He grunted and groaned and pounded her fiercely until her body was just wave after wave of pleasure.

It was so much. Too much? *No. Never.*

When he finally groaned his release, she was sure she would pass out from it all.

She collapsed forward and he slipped out. She heard him remove the condom she hadn't even known he'd put on, then he shifted down next to her, breathless.

"I like your kind of punishment," she all but purred. That had been the best damn experience of her adult sexual life. Totally unexpectedly hot.

"You're full of surprises, Missy."

She laughed. "I am?"

"Your body is so responsive." He slipped his arm around her and used his other hand to untie her wrists. "You're so damn sexy."

Once her hands were free, she ran them over his chest. "So are you."

"There's so much I want to do with you."

She hid her face against his chest because she didn't want him to see how much she wanted him to tell her he was falling for her again. "Me too."

Chapter Fifteen

"We can continue to fuck out your revenge as long as you'd like." Adam was lying on his back, one arm over his face, panting and feeling really fucking good.

Missy laughed then smacked his chest, jolting him so that he dropped his arm to look at her.

"I need you to know that I never forgot what I said to you. That day was a shitty one, and not just because of how I treated you."

"Well, you were awfully broody that day." She was grinning, letting him know that she wasn't still pissed off with him, at least not right now. No, right now she probably felt totally vindicated and, he was sure, very satisfied.

"For what it's worth, I'm sorry. I was a self-centered jerk back then and I didn't consider what my words would do to you. I mean, I actually kind of thought you could handle anything a dick like me could throw at you. You were always so tough."

"It was a long time ago." She rolled onto her back and let out a long breath, fluttering some hair out of her face in the process. "I'm over it."

Adam didn't believe that, not for a second. She didn't trust him enough to be honest right now, but that was okay. She didn't know him. Not really.

"I probably should have taken the cues and left you alone. You were looking all sulky. I mean, more than usual." She turned to look at him. "And I started talking to you, asking what was wrong with you. Maybe I wasn't being overly sensitive. I knew you wanted to be alone, but I didn't care."

"Yeah, but I chose to go to a public place. It's a free country. You had every right to be there." He sighed. "The reason why I remember that day so vividly is because my dad and I had had a fight. He'd kicked me out for the millionth time." Adam shook his head when her smile faded. "We never got along, so getting kicked out was like a weekly occurrence. But that time I had a place to go."

"New York." Missy nodded too. "I found out from your mom later that week."

"I remember you coming down to fish that day. You had your rod and tackle box. I should have left, let you have your time by the river in peace. My mind was on other things, though, so I didn't realize I wasn't fit to be around other people. I didn't really think much about how I must have hurt your feelings when I lashed out at you." He cringed. "Tough girl or not, I shouldn't have said what I said."

Missy shrugged one shoulder. "I think I might have blown it out of proportion a bit. I was pretty self-absorbed back then too. Like I said, I didn't even clue in that I should have left you alone—or maybe it was more like I didn't want to leave you alone." Her cheeks flared red. "Anyway, I'm sure you knew that I had the biggest crush on you back then."

"What? You don't anymore?" He nudged her with his arm, then pulled her closer so he could kiss her. "I didn't mean what I said, not the way I said it anyway. And I guess I always considered you my little friend. I didn't really see you as the grown-up version you are now. I missed the potential that was there, I guess."

"You were way older and cooler, and it was stupid for me to even think—"

"Not stupid. The timing just wasn't right then." He nuzzled her neck. "But the timing is perfect now." He pulled back so he could look at her. "I'm sorry, Missy, for hurting your feelings so badly back then. Obviously, I was a total loser for not seeing how amazing you are."

She ducked her head and burrowed against his chest, then wrapped her arms around his waist. "No, you were right. I wasn't much to look at back then. And all you did was tell me the truth. I needed a shower. I needed to brush my hair and, most likely, my teeth. I needed to start taking care of myself if I wanted a guy like you to notice me."

"I was truly a dick." Her agreeing with him only made him feel worse about it. "I should never have said that to you."

"Yeah, but in a way I needed to hear it, you know?" She kissed his chest and the gesture surprised him. All this tenderness she was showing… It was like she was a different person right now. Her defenses were down and he'd give anything to keep them that way. "After that day, and after you left, I kind of made it a mission to prove you wrong." She chuckled. "I had a picture of you on my treadmill."

"So I *was* motivational." He hugged her closer. He loved the feel of her in his arms. His mind was cycling through all the possible things he could say to fuck this up right now. *Stay cool, Lancaster. Stay cool.* "So that night at the party…"

"Yeah, it was quickly planned. I heard you were back in town and knew it was my chance."

"You got all dressed up so I wouldn't recognize you."

"And then we…well…did it."

"Pretty brave of you, Missy. Bold and daring too, for someone who likes following the rules—"

She pulled back so she could look up at him. "For some reason, when I'm with you, I feel not so bound by the rules, like it's okay to break a few of them, to take some risks. I don't know if that's a good or bad thing."

"I guess it depends on what's going on and what you're doing, but I'm glad that you're comfortable enough to be that way with me."

He could tell that she hadn't thought of it like that, but the way he figured it, a part of her was comfortable enough with him to have lowered her boundaries like she had time and time again when it came to sex. He just needed to figure out how to keep it that way.

He knew it was hard for her to set aside her usual protocol too. She pulled away from him so she could dangle over the side of the bed to retrieve her phone, giving him the most spectacular view of her ass.

"Lacey texted." She turned her screen for him to see as she settled back next to him.

The men were still drinking in the pub.

"So we're stuck here for a bit." He liked the stolen time and wished he could have more of it.

"I'm technically off duty for the night, but my deputy, Steve, knows he can reach me on my phone if there's an emergency." She put the phone on the nightstand and Adam could practically feel the unease starting to sink in for her. He knew she was itching to get back to law and order.

"You really are something special, Missy. I love that you went along with things today. Totally spontaneous. Best afternoon of killing time I've ever done. Beats being in New York any day."

She was quiet for a few minutes and he felt like maybe she would relax again, but then she tensed up and pulled back, and he got the feeling that her brain was working overtime, that or he'd just said something to set her off. The spell was slipping and he was losing this version of Missy.

"What about Sabine?" She put more distance between them and started grabbing for the blanket to cover herself. She was agitated, her face flushed.

"My boss?" She was more than his boss, sure. She was also his friend, but he felt like he needed to set some context for Missy.

"Your boss? You and she are together, aren't you? Fuck, I can't believe I forgot about that. What was I thinking?"

"Whoa, calm down." He tried to reach for her but she yanked her arm away and glared at him.

"Don't tell me to calm down. Doesn't it bother you that we cheated —"

"Hang on now." He pushed himself up. "Sabine and I aren't a couple."

Missy stopped her frantic scrambling and looked at him. "But the media says — "

He snorted. "The fucking media says a lot of things. Most of it is untrue." He rubbed the back of his neck. "I'm not going to lie. Sabine and I have been...well... intimate over the years. She's been a good friend to me as well, though. And I'm loyal to her — but not like you're thinking."

"So the media wasn't lying about the two of you hooking up."

"No, but we're not together. Never will be. She's got her man, whom she loves, and she's got me, the entertainment." It sounded harsh. "But not in a bad way. We have fun together."

"Oh." She rubbed her hand over her face. "Friends with benefits."

"At times, yes." He leaned toward her, one hand on her arm. "Does that bother you?"

She shrugged a shoulder. "I guess I have some insecurities about Sabine and the Kitty Cats."

"I'm not going to lie to you. I've had a lot of fun with many of the girls over the years. With Sabine too, but that's all it ever was." He reached for her and this time she didn't resist. "But, Missy, while I respect them all, they're not the type of women who are looking for a permanent relationship — not with me and not right now, anyway. Sabine isn't for me. She isn't who I'd want to settle down with."

Missy frowned. "Wait...! You'd want to settle down? Give up your fancy life in New York?"

"Hmm, not give up. I wouldn't expect you to give up your life here." He wrapped his arms around her and brought her head against his chest. She relaxed into him and that made him happy. "But I definitely want to change my life enough so that you're in it."

"Like a long-distance booty call?"

He laughed. "No, like a relationship—like a monogamous relationship, just you and me, if that's what would make you comfortable. To see what may happen. To maybe explore our boundaries and push past them a little." Monogamy was what he wanted and he guessed that Missy wouldn't be the type of woman to share him with someone else.

"Like a trial run."

He pulled her back enough to look her in the eyes. "Missy, I'm falling for you. Truly, I am." He bit his lip and held his breath, expecting her to pull away again.

She did freeze, tensing up for only a moment before she let out a deep sigh. "Yeah, I guess I am too." He knew that was hard for her to admit and he pulled her back into his chest so he could hug her again.

"We've known each other our whole lives. We come from the same place. There's something happening here. You feel it, right?"

She nodded.

"So let's see where this will go. Let's make room in our lives for each other."

She ran her hand over the plain of his chest. "Okay."

"Okay? That's all you have to say?" He laughed as he pulled her back so he could look into her eyes again.

"Okay, let's make room for each other and see what happens." She sighed again. "I'm not going to lie. This scares the hell out of me, but I can't deny that I want you in my life and I'm tired of trying to fight that."

He pressed his lips to hers, gently, tenderly, and as lust swept through him once again, his cock stirring to attention, he deepened the kiss, probing her with his tongue, getting tangled up. She slipped her hand around his back to rest against his ass and she encouraged him to slip inside her hot little pussy.

This was pure bliss and something he could get used to.

He rolled his hips slowly, savoring every second of being inside her. As she moaned her pretty little sounds and arched so that her nipples pressed against his chest, he pulled her even closer and found himself thinking that maybe, just maybe, he'd be able to convince Missy that they could make this work. He wanted it, and he was certain that she did too. It all felt pretty close to perfect.

Chapter Sixteen

Missy loved the feel of Adam's big body pressed against her. He was so huge that it was hard to even get her legs wrapped around his waist. Every stroke he gave her, each time his cock pressed deeply into her, she felt like she would spontaneously come. The constant rubbing against her clit, along her G-spot, it was the most amazing sensation she'd ever felt. She was learning just how many times she could come in a day. And it was a whole lot.

Her body felt satiated as the last of her climax rolled through her, so intense that she was out of breath for a while just lying with Adam. It was scary how easily she could get used to this — and not just because she craved his body like an addict with a drug. Adam was big and strong, imposing, but he was also sweet and tender. When he kissed her like he was now, he put everything into it, she could tell. He was falling for her and she couldn't deny her feelings were there too. No more anger, no more revenge. She was all in with Adam.

What had changed? Nothing, really. She'd just stopped fighting it. She'd always wanted Adam's attention and now she had it. Why give that up if she didn't have to?

It was close to midnight by the time Missy and Adam stepped outside Lacey's. The town was quiet. Only a few cars were on the roads. Missy loved this time of night. It made her feel like the town was at peace…and before Rex and his guys had come to Grimshield, it usually was.

They'd already said their goodbyes a few times and she didn't want to make a big deal about their parting, especially since it wouldn't be for very long. She felt good about that. No matter what happened next, she knew that her issues with Adam had been set aside and a new understanding had taken hold. They could be friends, maybe more than friends, and that was okay with her for now.

Missy had walked over to Lacey's rather than park her patrol vehicle there and draw more suspicions, and even though Adam had offered to drive her back to the office, she'd chosen to walk back instead. The night was cool, with a slight breeze and the scent of a campfire happening somewhere. She'd used to love that when she had been a kid. The crackling of the wood, the smell of burning logs mingling with whatever she was cooking on the fire. It was a huge part of her childhood. So the walk was refreshing and also gave her a chance to clear her head and set some goals. She needed to figure out if there was any way Elton Morrow could be creating a network for his trafficking enterprise. She needed to check in with her deputy, Steve, and make sure all was well in town.

As she neared the vehicle, she could hear the crackling of her radio through the closed window.

"Sheriff Alderton, you there? I need you to pick up. Sheriff?"

She frowned. She hadn't told Steve where she would be, but he did know that she wasn't taking a radio. If he needed her, he knew to call her cell. He wasn't the brightest bulb but he knew her protocol when she was technically off duty. *Keep me in the loop at all times.*

She opened her truck and got in, picking up the mic at the same time. "Deputy Webber, I'm here. What's your status?"

"Oh, Sheriff, thank God! There's a fire!"

"Where?" She looked in the direction that the breeze was coming from. The smoke she'd smelled wasn't from a campfire. She pulled herself fully into the truck, closed the door and turned the ignition.

"It's out on Concession Road 12, the Lancaster ranch. One of the barns is on fire. I called Hockly fire service but it's going to take twenty minutes for them to come."

Fuck! Grimshield had lost municipal funding a year ago when the county commissioner had decided that it would be better to concentrate all of the money on one huge fire service for three towns in a kind of amalgamation deal that was more about appearing innovative and cost-effective. In reality, it was about cutting short on fire protection and putting people in danger. While there was a fire truck that was supposed to be stationed in Grimshield, it was rarely there, being diverted to the other two bigger towns more frequently. It was the same reason she had trouble keeping a deputy. The county commissioner had amalgamated the funding to the sheriffs' offices too.

Now all the resources seemed to go to hiring law enforcement for the bigger of the towns, leaving Missy to make do with one deputy. When she'd demanded more, after Rex and his crew had arrived, she had been told to just deputize a few civilians if things got out of control.

"Okay, is the family out of the house?" Adam was on his way back there. She had to warn him.

"They're out and trying to rescue the horses."

"Got it! I'll be there in less than five!" She dropped the mic and turned on her sirens, then hit the gas.

She dialed Adam's number and put the phone to her ear. He didn't answer. She tried again.

He picked up after the third ring. "I know. I'm almost there." He didn't sound panicked or hysterical. He just sounded like he'd get things done. "We've got hoses on the property for this. We can pump from the river."

"The fire trucks are on their way." She hoped. "And so am I."

He grunted something that sounded like 'good' or 'okay'. It was hard to make out, then he was gone.

She threw her phone onto the passenger seat and focused on getting to the ranch in one piece.

The fire was almost at the point of raging out of control and looked like it was on its way to fully engulfing the biggest of the horse barns.

Missy helped move horses into the farthest paddock with Sally Lancaster and some of the farm hands while the rest of the men focused on the fire.

They had three hoses that were pumping huge amounts of water from the Shield, working hard to stop the fire from spreading and attempting to contain it to the one barn.

The air was thick with smoke and filled with the sound of terrified animals. Missy was pretty scared herself, because even though the fire was being brought to heel, she knew that those kinds of flames could be deceiving. She didn't want anyone getting hurt.

She could see Adam holding one of the ranch's hoses and aiming it at the heart of the flames. It looked effortless for him as he moved the pumping water where it needed to go. That gave her some comfort. As long as she got her eyes on him when she searched him out, she felt okay, and that was a curious emotion for her. After years of suppressing her feelings, she felt them bubbling to the surface more often. Adam, it seemed, was in her heart. She had to wonder if he had been in her heart the whole time, and not just as a focus of her sexual obsession.

There was a shout. Adam turned toward the farm hand next to him and motioned to his hose. The water was slowing almost to a trickle. Adam was shouting back, gesturing for the guy to pull the lever back harder. They needed all three of those hoses going or the fire was going to leap back up.

Missy was ready to leave the horses and go to help, but Adam passed his hose to the other guy then disappeared into the darkness toward the river.

Sally was shouting for Missy to help her corral two horses that were freaking out and get them into a fenced-in area farther away from the flames and separated from the other, calmer horses, lest they start a riot among the beasts. By the time Missy had helped get the animals under control, Adam was back, looking wet but unhurt. The hose that had been stopped up was flowing freely once again and Adam aimed it at the fire.

By the time the fire trucks arrived, there was little left but smoldering wood, which Fire Rescue took care of in a matter of minutes.

"Did you see what happened, Sally?" Missy asked once they finally had a chance to catch their breaths.

Sally had soot streaked all over her face, her hair was shooting out in all directions and she was wearing a nightgown that was covered in mud. Obviously she'd been pulled right out of bed when the alarm sounded.

"No, I didn't see anything but the fire." She was shaking her head, her eyes unfocused and her body trembling.

Missy reached out to her to steady her, scared that the woman was in shock and might collapse.

"I heard some shouting—or I think I did. That's what woke me up, shouting from the yard, then I saw the flickering coming through the window and I got up to see what was happening. That's when I saw the fire." She paused. "I saw Tommy. He was there."

A paramedic came over. "Are you okay, ma'am?"

Sally nodded but her eyes were still glassy.

"I think you need to check her out. She's unsteady."

Sally didn't argue. "We saved the horses. Right, Missy?"

Missy nodded. "They're all accounted for." She made sure to double-check with the ranch hands that every single horse had been pulled out of the barn, including the littlest one that had just been born the day before.

"You okay?" Adam came running to her, his chest heaving, his clothes covered in dirt and soot and even ripped or maybe burned in a few places.

"I'm okay. What about you, though?" She moved in close and pulled at some of the gaping holes in his shirt.

"Ouch, those look like burns, Adam. You need to see a medic."

"The Cooper boys did this," he growled, ignoring her concern over his obvious injury. "I need to head back into town."

"We don't know that for sure." Because they hadn't been paying attention to Rex and his men all night. They had been so preoccupied with their own fun and games. When Lacey's text had come, all it had said was *all clear*. It hadn't said why. Had Rex and his men still been at Lacey's when they'd left? Adam and Missy hadn't bothered to check. A wash of shame went through her. She'd been distracted.

That was why she didn't break protocol. That was what came from not following the rules. People could have been seriously hurt. Animals could have been killed.

Adam gave her a withering look. "They did this."

"But why would they? Don't they want the ranch?" It didn't make any sense. Why try to burn the place down if they wanted to buy the Lancasters out?

Missy pulled out her phone and texted Lacey.

Are Rex and his men at your place still?

"Fuck if I know why they'd start a fire! Maybe they're trying to scare my folks. Maybe they think that if the barn is destroyed, then Mom and Dad will want to sell or something."

Lacey's response vibrated her phone.

As far as I know, yes. Haven't seen any of them leave since they came back early from dinner.

She turned the phone toward Adam. "Rex and his men haven't left."

Adam opened his mouth to say something but was cut off by shouting.

"Tommy's missing," Denny Lancaster said. He was standing closer to what was left of the barn, looking around, seemingly frantic.

Adam gave Missy a look before running off toward the house. She watched him go inside and turn on all the lights as he searched for his brother. By the time he came back out, Missy had already guessed what he'd confirm.

"He's not in there."

Missy made her way to where Denny was standing. "Did you see Tommy tonight?" Sally had said the same thing.

Denny was only wearing a pair of track pants. His body was covered in black marks that were mixed with blood.

"You need to get treatment, Denny." Missy waved to the paramedics, who were just finishing up with Sally and the ranch hands. "Over here. These men need a check-up."

"Tom was here." Denny nodded. His eyes were glassy, just as Sally's had been, and he was darting them all over, maybe hoping to find Tommy among the men who were walking this way and that.

"Was he with anyone?" Missy looked over at Adam as he got within hearing range.

"I was just fallin' asleep when I heard shouting. Tommy and maybe other voices. I thought he was just blowing off steam like he does."

You mean when he's drunk and disorderly. Missy didn't say it out loud but she knew how belligerent Tommy could get after an all-night bender, and she had a theory forming in her brain that put Tommy and his new friends at the center of this particular investigation, just as Adam had suspected, but with a twist. Missy was fairly certain that Rex had already called in his *family*.

"But then the fire started and we were all out here knocking it down. I didn't see Tommy... He was nowhere."

Adam snapped his head toward the barn. They all did. *Ah shit*, she hadn't thought of that. The guy was a nuisance, but she didn't want him dead.

Adam took off running.

Missy followed him. "You can't go in there. It's not safe."

But he just kept running. His dad was right behind them, shouting, "You think he's in there, Adam? Is he in there? Tom! Tommy! Son! Call out if you're hurt!"

It was a desperate wail, a heartbreaking sound of panic as Denny followed Adam into the barn. Missy came to a skidding halt just outside the blackened, crumbled wood frame of the entrance. The firemen weren't expecting Adam and Mr. Lancaster to go running in, but they were prepared for Missy. They stopped her from following the men inside.

"It's not safe," one of them said.

"I know! But you just let those two men run in." She pointed behind him.

The guy just shook his head, as if she didn't get it somehow. "You're not going in. What's left of the roof could come down at any second."

"I'm the fucking sheriff!"

"Sheriff" — Ted Becks, the fire chief of Hockly, came walking out of the barn — "there are two men inside saying that a fellow named Tom is missing."

"Yes, Tommy Lancaster. This is his family's ranch. He's not in there, is he?"

"The damage is mainly to the back of the barn and the roof, and there are no bodies inside, ma'am," Ted said. "You might want to look into him being a missing person."

Adam and Denny came out of the barn, both with different expressions on their face — one a look of annoyance and frustration while the other looked only relieved. She wondered how relieved Denny would feel when he found out that Tommy had likely started the fire — or at least hadn't done anything to stop it from happening. *What the hell is Tommy playing at?*

"Hey, fellas, can I get your word that you'll stay outta there until we clear it?" Ted said as they passed the now-cordoned-off area.

"Of course, sorry." Adam nodded at Missy as he walked past her, his father right behind him.

"I'll file a preliminary report with you tomorrow afternoon, Sheriff. I should have some answers about origins and whatnot by then," Ted said.

Missy had her eyes on the Lancasters, watching as Denny stormed after Adam. She could practically feel the tension rising.

They made it about ten feet when Denny started yelling. "This is all your fault, Adam."

"Hang on a minute, Ted." She turned toward Adam, ready to intervene if needed.

Adam and his dad were facing off with one another. Adam was clenching his hands by his sides, like he was restraining himself. His father was poking a finger at his chest, trying, no doubt, but failing, to move his brick wall of a son.

"You have always been trouble for this family, Adam." He made no attempt to lower his voice. It was like he wanted an audience. "You're a disgrace. Your lifestyle is disgusting and now you're here causing more trouble for us."

Adam's jaw was clenched so tight that Missy thought he might bust some teeth. She wanted to step in, to come to Adam's defense, but she knew there was nothing she could say that would stop this shitshow from going down. Emotions were running high right now.

"You've probably been meddling in things, right? Your ma said you were here to investigate... Well, take a look at what your investigating has led to." He waved his arm toward the barn. "You pissed those guys off and they've done this."

Missy looked around to see that everyone was trying hard not to make it obvious that they were listening.

Adam didn't say a word, but she could tell just by the slight curve of his shoulders that he was taking all this in and maybe starting to believe that it was all his fault. He looked defeated, like he was ready to give up, like he'd taken one too many hits.

"And now Tommy is missing because of you," Denny snarled.

Missy stepped in. She couldn't help herself. "Hey now, Denny, Mr. Lancaster." She slipped in beside Adam, letting her arm brush against his. "You know just as well as I do that Tommy likes to disappear without letting anyone know where he's gotten to. He disappeared for a year, not too long ago. Remember? I tracked him down to Mexico and there he was, have a great time."

Denny was glowering at her, his glare like hot pokers. She didn't flinch. She'd spent months trying to track Tommy down, spent hours of time searching and calling in favors that she'd probably never be able to repay. Then she'd hired a PI to do the tracking until finally she'd found him with Elton Morrow, and she'd known then that he was into some shady shit.

"I've spent a lot of time tracking Rex and his men, doing some research into where they came from. They always seem to leave a path of destruction no matter where they go." Okay, they'd never started a fire per se, but they had caused damage in several towns they'd stayed in. "Adam didn't bring this on." She waved her hand toward the barn. "This is just collateral damage to something much, much bigger. And Tommy is at the center of it all."

Adam was staring at her. She kept her eyes on Mr. Lancaster.

"Tommy made a deal with a criminal, a guy named Elton Morrow, then attempted to renege on it." That was what she'd pieced together from her own investigation. Tommy had made promises to Elton that his parents would sell their ranch, but things weren't working out the way he'd planned. "And now you are paying the price of that."

She hadn't told Adam any of this because she didn't want him to ask too many questions. When she shifted her eyes to his, though, she realized that he wouldn't have questions. He already knew — or at least he clearly suspected — enough to not be surprised.

Damn, the man was *that* good. She should give him a little more credit and partnered up with him before now.

"Tommy left with someone." Sally came into the conversation at that point, wrapping her arms around Denny as she did. "I saw him. He was here before the fire really got going. I was trying to throw the window open to shout at him, but he just got into a truck and drove away." She looked up at her husband, her eyes looking totally confused. "Why would he do that, Den?"

Adam looked over at Missy, his expression saying everything. "He's not the man you think he is," Adam said.

Sally looked over at him, the confusion clear on her face.

"I want you out of my sight," Denny growled. "I want you gone."

Missy wasn't sure if he meant her as well, but she took the cue and laid her hand over Adam's arm. "Come on. I'll take you back to my office. We can figure out what to do next from there."

She sure as shit knew one thing. It was time to start playing this game as a team. It was time to officially bring Adam in.

Chapter Seventeen

Adam went to get his things while Missy sorted out business. He could hear her blasting her deputy as Adam took two steps at a time up to the loft.

Adam's head was not in a good place. For one, he did feel responsible for the fire. If he'd been home, maybe he would have been able to stop it from even starting. What had happened between him and Missy had been reckless and distracting. He should have been paying attention to Rex's moves all night instead of drooling over Missy's. So yeah, he felt guilt. A lot of it.

Adam needed to keep his head in the game and get things done his way.

And that was the other reason Adam felt responsible. It was possible that Rex had figured out Adam was surveilling them. Maybe he'd found one of the bugs Adam had planted or maybe he'd sussed out somehow that the computers were corrupted.

Whatever it was, Adam had a feeling that Rex knew enough to keep his men at Lacey's while he sent out others to do his dirty work. Despite his threats the previous day to Missy that he was going to call in his family, Adam now believed Rex had already brought in reinforcements to stir up shit. Rex was trying to pull Adam's attention in different directions and it didn't help that he'd been so distracted by Missy. So yeah, in a way it was his actions that had brought the fire on, just like his father had said. And maybe they were better off without him meddling.

As soon he made it up to the loft and saw the state of his room, he had his confirmation. Rex knew about the surveillance. Adam's computers, both of them, were trashed and the room was ripped apart.

He knew Tommy had had a hand in this, just like he knew that what Missy had said was true. Tommy had made a deal and it had gone south somehow. Maybe he'd bragged about the location of his parents' ranch. Maybe he'd been in on the whole deal, using the river to transport product—because Adam was almost certain now that was what was going on.

He grabbed his duffel and threw a few things in. He didn't need his computers to access his feeds, so it didn't matter that they'd been smashed. He could log in to the program he used from any computer and his team was recording everything to the Cowan database anyway.

He dialed work. Brett, his second in command, picked up. "Yo, boss, what's up?"

"How's the feed looking on my special project?"

Bret clicked away for a second or two before answering. "Computers are not active. You want me to turn them on?"

"Do it." Adam zipped up his duffel then scanned the room one last time.

"Rooms are empty, not a person in sight. Interesting, though... I see cell phones, probably burners, piled up on the table."

Fuck. "Okay, thanks, Bret. You can kill the feeds now." Rex and his guys had somehow figured it all out. Adam wasn't going to be getting any new intel from their devices. Missy had warned him that Rex was always one step ahead and Adam hadn't listened.

"You got it, boss. Need anything else from me tonight?"

"We're good." The tech side of things was a bust and Adam had fucked up, but that didn't mean he was out of the game.

Missy was waiting for him in her truck by the time he made it back downstairs.

"My deputy is staying here to hold the scene. I need to get back to the office so I can make a few calls."

"You think you could make those calls from the riverside out by the old bridge?"

Missy frowned. "Yeah, I can get a signal there just as well as anywhere else."

"Good, I need you to take me there first."

* * * *

The old bridge had collapsed about forty years before and had never been rebuilt. It was mainly used as a drinking hideaway for the older kids in town at night and one of the favorite places for the younger kids to catch fish and swim. Adam always liked to go there to think when the sun was just about to set, and there was usually no one around. When he thought about his reasons for missing Grimshield, it was this spot that his mind went to first.

"You gonna tell me what we're doing here?" Missy put the truck in park but Adam was already getting out.

"Make your calls. I'll just be a second." He knew this area like the back of his hand and moved with confidence, despite the fact that the sky was still dark — not midnight-dark, but dark enough that Adam wasn't worried about being seen.

"Adam, wait." Missy put her hand on his arm to stop him from jumping out.

"Missy, I'm not going to do anything illegal." *Probably.*

She rolled her eyes. "Adam Lancaster, with the power vested in me as the Sheriff of Grimshield, Montana, I hereby deputize you. You are now a civilian law enforcement officer working under my protection and jurisdiction."

Adam could have dropped dead from shock. "Um…what?"

She nodded once. "You're my deputy and I'm officially assigning you to this investigation. Now anything you have to do is sanctioned."

Adam liked the way she was thinking. "Good. I'll be right back."

The river was moving at a good clip this time of year and the sound of the water rushing over the rocks and against the banks was both familiar and comforting. It also guided him right to where he needed to be.

He could hear Missy's muffled voice as she got out of the truck, presumably to follow him. She was speaking to whomever she'd needed to contact. He worked his way in close enough to the water's edge that the spray was hitting his face here and there, then he turned the flashlight on his phone on and directed it to the center of the water flow.

It took him exactly three seconds to find what he was looking for.

When the hose had stopped working back at the ranch, he'd gone to the pumps by the river to see what was going on. There were three intake valves that sucked water from the Shield and diverted them to the hoses. Adam had had to get into the water to see anything, but when he did, he'd realized that something was blocking one of the valves. With a bit of tugging, he'd pulled the blockage out. It was a thick black balloon, the kind made out of strong latex that was sometimes used on weather balloons. It had no business being in the river, but as soon as he'd found it, he'd realized what Rex and his crew were up to — or at least he'd suspected. Now he had confirmation.

Elton Morrow wasn't sending boats up the river with product. No, that would be too obvious. He was sending inflatables. Adam could make out the mini rafts that weren't big enough to hold a person but were probably stuffed full of some kind of illicit drug. And they weren't merely moving with the river. They were staying on course, dead center, practically invisible due to all the black material, especially if a person wasn't looking for them.

He had to get a closer look.

He was just dropping his pants when he heard the crunch of Missy's approach. "Jesus, you do like getting naked, don't you?" The beam of her flashlight hit his bare ass and, he hoped, gave her a great view. "What in the world are you doing?"

Adam stripped his shirt off, gave her a salute then waded into the river. And… "Fuck!" It was cold! Way colder than he ever remembered it being.

"We've had the spring run-off draining from the mountains all summer. The Shield is way below temp, Adam." Missy's voice sounded half concerned, half bewildered. "You sure you want to go in for a dip?"

Adam cursed his way in, fighting against the current and the ball-freezing temps to get to one of the mini rafts.

As soon as Missy realized where he was headed, she shone her light at the nearest target. "What the hell are those?" And as she trailed along the line of them…at least five in this part of the river, he heard her gasp. "Holy shit, are those what I think they are?"

Adam had one in his gasp. "The damn thing has a powerful motor on it. Probably guided by satellite." He didn't want to lift the thing out of the water for fear that Rex and his men were monitoring movement, so he guided it off course, working against whatever signal it was getting. "There's a knife on my belt. Grab it, would ya?"

Missy dropped down, almost out of sight as Adam fought to bring the raft closer to the bank.

"T-t-toss it-t-t." His teeth were chattering so hard that his words came out kind of stunted. His whole body felt frozen and his muscles were cramping.

Missy did as he asked then turned and took off up the embankment. "I'm getting a blanket. You get out of that water before you freeze to death."

Adam somehow managed to catch the knife and work his fingers to open it. The raft's motor was making a whirring whine that was getting louder by the second. He slit along the top of the thick rubber and, sure enough, a puff of white came out. He reached in and pulled out a kilo of powder.

Rex was moving product up the Shield. He wanted the land so that he'd have a distribution channel that likely wouldn't be monitored. Lancaster ranch was smack dab in the middle of the Shield's track and would allow for monitoring as the rafts moved along the river. This was what Rex was doing with the properties he was acquiring.

"Adam, get out of that water! I swear you look pale as a ghost right now." Missy was back with a giant blanket open and waiting for him.

He held up the kilo. "We just got an assload of evidence." His whole body was trembling so hard that he thought he might collapse.

"Adam, get out of there."

"Yes, Mr. Lancaster, please do get out of there. You're holding up my production line." Rex stepped out of the shadows, flanked by two of his men. They both had shotguns aimed directly at the back of Missy's head. The threat was clear.

Missy released the blanket she was holding and went for her gun.

"Uh-uh, Sheriff. Hands behind your head if you please."

One of his men pumped his gun. Missy froze, darting her gaze to Adam.

Adam raised his hands, kilo and all, and shook his head. His body was vibrating hard now, partly from the freezing cold temps of the water and partly from the shot of adrenaline rushing through his veins.

"You can't possibly think—" Missy started.

"Sheriff," Rex cut her off, "when will you realize that you don't have control here? Hands behind your head."

"Missy, please," her deputy said as stepped out from behind one of Rex's guys. "Just do as he says." He had a zip tie in his hand as he approached Missy.

"So you *are* connected in all this shit." Missy spat, turning her eyes back to Adam. "That call I made? I got confirmation that my deputy is related to our county commissioner. His nephew."

"Deputy Webber has been my eyes and ears for as long as he's been under your leadership. He blends into the walls, doesn't he? Perfect for eavesdropping and spying on an unaware, cocky sheriff. He wisely tagged your vehicle with a tracker months ago and alerted me when you parked here. You should know that you can't make a move or a call in this town without me knowing about it," Rex said.

It all made sense to Adam now. Her deputy was a plant, put in place to keep an eye on Missy. It was possible he'd bugged her office and her phone. That was likely how Rex seemed to know things he shouldn't. Adam could tell by Missy's expression that this realization was dawning on her too.

"The good commissioner offered up his nephew to keep an eye on things while we got our operation underway." Rex snorted. "I would have like to just dispose of you, replace you with another, more obliging sheriff, but Commissioner Richardson said you were just a small-town girl, too stupid to really figure out what was going on."

Missy bristled, her shoulders tensing and fists clenching. She wasn't moving her arms up—she was moving them toward her gun again. Adam could see her mind working as her deputy approached. She wouldn't let this slide.

She was going to get herself killed.

"Let her go and I'll help you expand your distribution lines," Adam blurted.

Missy froze and whipped her head toward him, her eyes full of shock. "Adam—" Her deputy ran at her, taking her out at the knees so she dropped hard to the ground.

Adam tried to jump out of the water but his legs refused to move properly, so he only managed to stumble a few steps forward.

"I wouldn't do that if I were you." One of Rex's men shifted his gun to point at Adam's chest.

Adam's whole body was shaking and his lips chattering. He couldn't feel his lower body. He needed to get the fuck out of the water before he passed out.

Missy was on her stomach, her arms secured behind her back and her gun gone from her holster.

"You look cold, Adam," Rex said. "Why don't you come out of that water and explain to me how you think you can help me move my product."

Adam forced himself to move. One slow step at a time, he finally got out of the freezing water. The warm air did nothing to bring feeling back to his legs.

"Deputy, give Adam that blanket, would you? Now tell me, Adam. Does this offer have anything to do with your boss, the esteemed Ms. Cowan?"

The deputy jumped away from Missy to do his boss's bidding, offering the blanket she had dropped to Adam with shaking hands.

"You know it does and you know that she has a previous relationship with your boss, Elton Morrow." Adam snatched it out of the deputy's hands and wrapped it around his body, taking momentary comfort as it wicked away the water and gave him back a bit of heat. He could feel Missy's eyes on him, blasting him with confusion. "But before we get into that, I need to know where my brother is."

"Your brother caused quite a problem for me at your family's ranch. He thought he'd deter us from our plan by setting the place on fire. Doesn't really think things through, does he?"

Adam couldn't begin to understand why Tommy would do something so damn stupid, but confirmation that he'd started the fire didn't surprise Adam. "Where is he now?"

"We have him in a safe place. Luckily he didn't impact our current shipment from continuing on to its destination." Rex motioned to the kilo in Adam's hand. "Although you, on the other hand, have cut into some of our profit." Rex laughed darkly as he motioned to one of his men. "Elton did mention his connection with your boss Sabine. I can't say that ended particularly well, though, did it?"

"Sabine was a user back then. She had to cut ties so she could get clean. You know how successful she is now, and she's always interested in finding ways to make money. She's no stranger to back-door deals."

Missy's eyes went wide, staring up at him from where she lay on the dirt. He wished he could explain to her that this was the only way. If Sabine got involved, Missy would be safe. He'd get Rex to move the shipment line away from Grimshield and Missy wouldn't be stuck in the middle of this drug trafficking situation.

"Yes, I do know of Sabine's success in various illicit activities." Rex shook his head. "But my boss won't work with just anyone. He'll need some assurances."

"She'll give you those assurances. You know she's a professional. She always makes sure everyone leaves satisfied," Adam said.

Rex snorted. "So I've heard."

He motioned to his jeans. "You mind if I put some pants on?"

Rex eyed him for half a second before waving his hand. "Go ahead."

"If you cut Sabine in, she could move product for you." Move it right into the hands of the DEA. She had contacts in all the right places. He snatched his pants up and put them on. His phone was in his pocket. All he had to do was call Sabine and say one word. She'd know what to do. "I've already told her Elton is involved here." He did his pants up then pulled his phone out, unlocking the screen and hitting Sabine's number. "I'll give her a call so you can talk to her about the plans."

"I've got a better idea. Why don't we invite her here? That way she can be reunited with her old friend, Mr. Morrow. Thanks to Tommy, Elton is on his way to deal with the current situation."

Before Adam could make a move, his head was covered and he felt the bite of a taser, knocking him to his knees as pain ripped through his body. It only lasted a few seconds though, not enough to keep him down.

Rex snatched his phone and put it to his ear. "Ms. Cowan, my name is Rex Cooper and I've got a message for you from your old friend Elton Morrow."

Adam started to shout but his words were stripped from his throat when what felt like fifty thousand volts blasted him into unconsciousness.

Chapter Eighteen

Missy didn't understand how everything had gone sideways so quickly. After Adam had been knocked out, Rex and his men had quickly bound his hands with a zip tie then carted both of them off to a waiting van. They'd traveled to a barn she didn't recognize—not that she knew all the insides of all the barns in the county, but it had taken them at least thirty minutes to drive to wherever they were. If she were going to guess, she'd have thought they were in Hockly.

Once they'd arrived, both she and Adam had been tied to posts on opposites sides of the stable. Adam was still out cold and Missy's arms were all pins and needles. Rex and his goons had left the two of them alone in there for what seemed like hours.

She glanced over at Adam. He was slumped to the side, his big arms torqued behind him, his legs splayed out in front. She watched the rise and fall of his chest and was thankful he was still breathing.

Even if she wanted to kill him.

What had he been thinking? Trying to make a deal with Rex? Bringing Sabine into the conversation like he had it all worked out? Missy didn't know whether to be more angry or hurt. Was Adam really that comfortable with doing things on the shady side of business that he'd be willing to enter into a drug ring to protect Grimshield? Was his boss the kind of woman who would traffic drugs all over the country?

Missy's first instinct was to say yes. Sabine Cowan seemed to be exactly the type of woman to do something like that. She made money off the backs of her Kitty Cats—or at least that was what Missy had thought she did. Adam had said that she didn't exploit the women she employed, but after what had just happened, how easy it had been for Adam to try to wheel and deal in the name of his boss... Well, Missy didn't know what to believe.

Adam moaned and Missy snapped her eyes into focus just in time to see his head bob.

"Adam," Missy whispered hoarsely. "Adam, wake up!"

His head lolled to the other side.

"Adam!" She raised her voice as high as she dared, not wanting to call attention to them. She didn't know how close Rex and his men were, and she didn't want to alert them to Adam waking up.

Adam's head snapped up as he sucked in a deep breath. "Missy?" He whipped his head around until his gaze landed on her. "Are you okay? Did they hurt you?"

She shook her head. They'd hurt her pride maybe but not her body. "I'm okay. How do you feel?"

He grunted. "Like I was electrocuted."

"Right about now would be a good time for you to use your handy zip-tie-breaking trick." Missy nodded toward the end of the barn. "They've checked in once in the time we've been here, however long that's been." The barn was windowless and the barn lights were blazing, so if she were to guess by the level of her exhaustion, she'd put them somewhere a little north of daybreak.

"How long have I been out?"

Missy tried for a shrug. "A while." Long enough for her to be worried that he might never wake up, not long enough to forgive him for turning traitor.

"Have you seen Tommy?"

Missy sighed. "No."

He shifted his body, moving his shoulders, trying to pull his bound arms around the side of the post he was attached to. Nothing seemed to be working the way he wanted it to, though. When he pulled one way with his arms, his body moved the other way. They had not only tied his wrists together behind the pole but they also seemed to have attached his wrist bindings to the pole. He couldn't do much more than shift one way or the other.

After a few minutes of trying, he finally let out a rough sigh and let his arms relax. "Fuck! I can't break these ties."

She slumped against her pole, feeling defeated once again. "So what do we do?"

"I don't know. I need time to think."

Missy let the silence hang for less than a minute before she couldn't wait any longer. "Will Sabine come here? Will she make a deal with Elton?" Would she trade Adam's life for an agreement to traffic drugs? Would she let Rex and the gang get rid of the only sheriff in town? "I won't be bought, Adam, if that's what you think. I won't take one penny of your boss's money to stay quiet—"

"Missy, for fuck's sake!" Adam said. "Sabine isn't going to buy you off."

A lump the size of a walnut grew in Missy's throat. "So what? I'm just a liability. She'll get rid of me just like Rex was going to do?" Every single awful thing she'd heard about Sabine was front and center in her thoughts right now.

Adam shot her a hard look but he couldn't say anything more about that, because the double doors of the barn opened and Rex and his entourage walked in.

"Glad to see you awake, Adam," Rex's booming voice filled the open space. "I was getting worried that your little nap would having you missing the meeting between your boss and Mr. Morrow. Ms. Cowan insisted you be brought alive and unscathed."

Missy scanned the crowd, her eyes going wide when she saw Tommy standing at the back, his arms crossed. He didn't look hurt. He wasn't bound. He looked like one of the mob.

"Where's my brother?" Adam barked.

"As you can see, Tommy is alive and well." Rex motioned behind him. "Ready to accompany you to the meeting."

"Tommy, you hurt?"

Tommy stepped forward, a gun in his hands and pointed at Adam. "Not hurt. Untie him from the post. We have to go. But don't untie his wrists."

One of the other men came around the back of the post with a knife.

Despite knowing that she couldn't get out of the restraints—she'd been trying for the entire time there were in the barn—she tugged at the zip tie again anyway and winced when the flesh on her already sore wrist pulled painfully.

"Now, Tommy, remember… If you try any shit with Adam, I'm going to put a bullet into your pretty little sheriff's head." Rex didn't have a gun in his hand, but that didn't make Missy feel any better. She knew all he'd have to do was motion to one of his men and she was as good as dead.

"Like I already told you, Rex, I can't stand this motherfucker. I want him gone. The sooner he gets to his boss, the sooner I don't have to deal with him in my life." Tommy pushed his gun against the back of Adam's head. "If you try anything, Adam, I'm going to shoot you. Don't even test me on that."

Adam growled. Now that he was free from the post, Missy hoped Adam would be able to do his magic to break the zip tie.

"Hey, maybe you should put another zip tie on him," Steve, her former deputy said. "He broke out of the one we had on him at the station the other day."

Missy cursed under her breath. No way he'd be able to get out of two zip ties. He wasn't a superhero.

One of Rex's men strapped on another zip tie.

"Don't fuck this up like you fucked up the barn burn, Tommy," Rex said when Tommy leaned in to seemingly check that the zip tie was being put on properly.

Tommy snapped his head up and glared at Rex. "Fucker wanted to burn my folks' house down…while they were in it!"

That wasn't the story Rex had told back at the river. He'd made it seem like setting a fire at the Lancaster ranch had been all Tommy's idea.

"Eddie didn't apprise me of his plans," Rex said. "He got carried away."

And that sounded to Missy like Rex wasn't as in charge as he'd like everyone to think he was. If Eddie was from the extended family, he likely was taking orders directly from Elton Morrow.

"Carried away? That idiot is a pyromaniac! He could have killed someone," Tommy said.

"We needed your folks off that property. You suggested a fire. We did a fire." Rex shrugged.

"You son of a bitch!" Adam yelled. "I thought Rex was lying, but it really was your idea?"

Missy's stomach churned. How could Tommy do something like that?

"They wouldn't sell." Tommy shrugged. "I figured the insurance payout on top of what Elton is willing to pay would be enough to convince them. Besides, I knew Dad would get the fire under control with the hoses. Three of them pulling from the Shield was bound to get enough water for you to do something about it."

The brothers were toe-to-toe at this point and Missy watched as they glared for what seemed like an eternity, until she noted a slight change in Adam's expression. It was ever-so-slight and his shoulders eased minutely — but it was there. Tommy had sent him some kind of message. Missy was sure of it.

What in the world…? Had Tommy set the fire to draw Adam's attention to the river on purpose? Was it his attempt to clue Adam in to the drug rafts?

If that were the case, Tommy maybe wasn't as big an idiot as she had originally thought. What he'd done was damn stupid, yes, but maybe in his muddled brain, he'd thought he was doing something that would help.

And it had helped, just a little too late. There was nothing Missy could do about the drug rafts when she was tied up in a barn.

Adam turned to look at Rex but his gaze landed on her. "You do anything to the sheriff and you'll pay for it."

"No worries, Adam." Rex laughed as he walloped Adam on the back. "We won't touch a hair on her head...unless you give us a reason to. Now run along and help broker the deal between my boss and yours."

Adam was leaving and Missy would be on her own. She needed a plan. Quick. There was no way she was out of this game.

She tugged one more time on her restraints. *Ouch.* They weren't budging.

"Unlike Adam, I don't think you're strong enough to bust outta that zip tie, Sheriff," Rex said. "All the same... Steve, why don't you stay with her while we make sure Adam gets going without any trouble."

Her former deputy nodded. "No problem, Rex."

"Your uncle's gonna reward you for your service. You came through for us, boy." He patted Steve on the shoulder then winked at Missy. "Steve's been such a great source of information. I knew all your moves before you even made them." He looked back at Steve. "Make sure none of the guys touch her, would ya?" He winked at Missy like this was all some kind of joke.

She was gonna knock that guy on his ass the first chance she got.

"Sure thing." Steve put his gun back into his holster then crossed his arms before turning his back to her.

If her only protection was Steve, she was doomed.

They both watched Rex and his men leave, then she waited a heartbeat before speaking.

"You bugged my office? Tapped my phone?"

Steve ignored her.

"You slimy little puke, were you listening to all my conversations?"

His shoulders heaved.

"You're pathetic. And you're a disgrace, wearing that uniform like you deserve to." Missy was mad at herself too. She'd underestimated Steve *big* time. She should have clued in that he might be a plant, but how was she to have known that he was related to the commissioner? It had just been a hunch that'd had her looking for a connection between Steve and the powers-that-be. One of her law-enforcement contacts had confirmed his identity over the phone just before he'd outted himself at the riverbank, but there hadn't been enough time for her to have done anything about it.

"That's enough, Missy," Steve's voice quavered but he didn't look over his shoulder at her. "Keep quiet."

"It's *Sheriff* Alderton, and I won't keep quiet. You betrayed me, Steve. You betrayed the people of this town. How dare you!"

"Well, I'll be gone before you know it," Steve said, his voice low. "If your friend has his way, we won't be staying here, so don't you worry about me sticking around."

If my friend has his way? Adam was going to get rid of Rex and his gang by moving the operation into his boss's umbrella somehow. So he was saving her town but not saving himself. Not really. As much as that would solve her problem, it didn't work with her conscience or her feelings toward Adam. She didn't want him tangled up with Rex or Elton Morrow.

"You keep your mouth shut, Missy, and you may just get out of this with no harm done." He cocked an eyebrow in her direction. "You might just get a big fat paycheck for your trouble if you play your cards right."

Money? "I wouldn't touch your boss's filthy money with a ten-foot—"

"Be quiet already." Steve pulled his gun out and turned on her. His hand was shaking. "Shut up or I'll shut you up."

"You won't do that. You're too weak," she spat.

His eyes flashed and he moved toward her, waving the gun like an idiot. It was actually terrifying. "Maybe I'll make an example of you. Pay you back for all the times you were such a bitch to me."

He was being so 'big macho man' that he didn't realize how close he was to her. The second he got within reach, she kicked her foot out, taking him at the ankle so he fell sideways. The gun went flying as he tried to stop himself from falling on her. She raised her knee and got him square in the groin. He pitched forward and slammed his head against the pole, effectively knocking himself out in the process.

That couldn't have worked out more perfectly.

He was lying next to her, slumped on his side. She shifted her arms just as Adam had tried to do and managed to just barely swipe Steve's utility belt where his knife was. *Not quite close enough.* She hooked her leg around his waist, taking no pleasure in having to wedge herself against his ass to pull him closer. *One more inch...* She tugged and shifted, straining against the hard plastic of the zip tie and Steve's dead weight. Her heart was hammering. Sweat was beading. She just needed one more little bit. She yanked him another inch. Her fingers touched the metal but she couldn't get a grip on it.

She heard shouting outside the barn. A gun went off, then there was more shouting. *Fuck. Fuck. Fuck!* Something was happening out there.

She shifted herself again and used her foot to leverage against Steve's leg, hooking him in and nudging him closer until... *Yes!* She got it. One flick with her thumb and the knife was open. It took some awkward hacking, but she got herself free.

She grabbed Steve's gun, his extra magazine and a bunch of zip ties from his utility belt and started toward the barn doors. It was time for Rex to get what was coming to him.

Chapter Nineteen

Adam had to get back to Missy. That was priority number one. He didn't trust Rex or his men not to do something to her.

Tommy had Adam in his pickup with two other guys from Rex's crew, one sitting up front with Tommy and one in the back with him. They were driving down one of the many rural roads—headed to the highway, most likely, then to wherever the meeting was supposed to go down.

"Your boss's plane has landed," Tommy snarled, his eyes on Adam in the rear-view mirror. "She told Rex that the meeting would happen at the airport in a private hangar."

A private hangar. Right. He hadn't talked to Sabine himself, so he didn't know what the actual plan was, but he knew what meeting in a private hangar meant. She was setting the stage for some kind of take-down. Normally he'd be there with her, sussing out the meeting place, ensuring that there would be no way any harm could come to her, but obviously that wasn't possible this time. He trusted his security officers. He'd trained them all. They'd protect Sabine with their lives if necessary, just as he would. He wasn't worried about Sabine. She would be protected and she always had a plan. Elton Morrow was in for a world of hurt, one way or another.

"I hope she brought some of her Kitty Cats," the guy next to Adam said as he elbowed Adam's arm. "I've heard that those girls like to party."

Adam grunted but didn't trust himself to speak. He had to think. Sabine was expecting him to show up at the hangar, but she didn't know about Missy. She wouldn't have planned with the idea that she needed to protect the sheriff too.

Fuck. He needed to get back to that barn. He didn't trust Rex's family for one hot second not to move her to another location or rough her up.

"I've gotta piss," Adam growled.

"Hold it," the guy sitting up front barked.

"You asshole. I'm gonna piss all over the place back here. We've got an hour drive to the airport. You wanna be smelling piss the whole way?"

"No, we can stop." Tommy jerked the wheel, sending the truck roughly onto the shoulder. He caught Adam's eye in the rear-view and Adam gave a minute nod. This was going down right now and Tommy was in it with him.

Adam had realized when they were toe-to-toe in the barn that Tommy was on his side. Tommy had used his words intentionally. He'd thought the fire would alert Adam to the drug rafts. In his warped little brain, he'd thought he was solving a problem instead of creating one. But like most things Tommy tried to do, the timing had been way off and it hadn't gone down the way he'd thought it would.

Adam would hash out Tommy's stupidity with him later. For now, they needed to take out these guys and get back to the farm.

The truck came to an abrupt halt and Adam used the jostling movement to hook one of the zip ties onto the belt blades he had and snap it off. One gone, one to go.

Missy had wanted to know how he'd snapped those zip ties? All she'd had to do was inspect his belt for thirty seconds and she'd have found the small blades he had embedded in the leather. They notched up but lay flat until he needed them, then, with a little flip, they popped out and were ready to use. They were great for getting out of bindings. He never left the house without his belt on. No one would believe the number of times having belt blades had come in handy. Given Adam's line of work, he kept finding himself tied up, one way or another.

The guy sitting next to him opened the door and attempted to yank his arm. "Get out and be quick about it."

Adam started to slide toward the door. "You gonna take out my dick and hold it for me?"

The guy's eyes nearly bulged out of his head.

"Hey, what the fuck is this?" The guy sitting in the front was leaning over his seat, reaching for the broken zip tie.

Adam snapped the second tie with his belt blades, finally releasing his arms. Still half in and half out of the truck, he twisted his body slightly and took the guy waiting for him to get out by surprise with an uppercut to his jaw that sent him flying backward. Adam turned in time to see Tommy take the other guy out with an elbow to the face.

Within minutes they had both guys on their stomachs on the grass just off the gravel road, double zip ties binding their wrists. Adam dug into both mens' pockets, one after the other, to grab their phones.

"We have to go back for Missy." Adam motioned for Tommy to get into the truck as he moved around to the passenger side.

"You can't leave us here," one of the other guys shouted. "If we don't show to meet your boss, she's in for a world of hurt."

Adam snorted, rolled his eyes then leaned down so he could make eye contact. "My boss has friends in high places. She'll make sure someone finds you…eventually."

"What? You motherfucker! You can't leave us here!" One of the guys was grunting and rolling around, trying to get out of his zip tie.

"Enjoy the downtime." Adam got into the truck and shut the door. "Let's go."

Tommy turned the truck around and gunned it down the road, leaving a trail of gravel dust behind them.

Adam was on edge. He knew Sabine had things under control but he didn't know what to expect back at the farm. Missy was tied up. Defenseless. He needed to get her to safety. He checked the two phones he had in his hand. Both required thumb prints to access. "Give me your phone. Rex took mine."

Tommy didn't argue. He just reached into his pocket and pulled out his phone.

Adam dialed Sabine. The call went straight to voicemail.

He texted her instead. *It's Adam. I'm safe.*

"I didn't set the fire," Tommy blurted, his voice rough, staring straight ahead.

"But it was your idea." Adam didn't want to do this right now. Having it out with his brother always seemed to end in a fistfight. He needed to preserve his energy for whatever he was going to find at the farm.

"I knew you'd figure it out. You know, the drug rafts? I knew you'd see them in the Shield when you were getting the hoses on the fire. I planned it out so the timing would be right. I made sure to clog up that hose so you'd go out there. You're a smart guy. I knew you'd have it all under control and Rex would get what's coming to him."

"You took a massive risk. So many things could have prevented me from finding those rafts." Adam scoffed. "You could have killed someone just with the damn fire. The horses could have died. Any number of people could have been injured fighting that fire."

Tommy had the sense to look contrite. "I know. I realize that now. I was just desperate. Rex was talking about getting rid of Mom and Dad — you know, permanently — and I panicked. I figured a fire would scare them off and they'd get insurance money — "

"Tommy, you need to stop talking before I punch you in the mouth." Adam raised his hand when Tommy started to argue again. "We'll deal with this later." The farm appeared over the next hill. The loud *pop pop pop* of gunfire had Adam's hackles rising. "Oh fuck!" He had to get to Missy.

* * * *

Missy slipped out of the barn and immediately ducked low, pressing her back against the wall as she took in the surroundings. The sun was rising. Its rays were muted behind a graying, stormy-looking sky, but there was enough light to give her a good idea of what the layout of the farm was. There were dark shadows everywhere, which worked in her favor. She stuck to them as she moved to the end of the barn wall and slowly rose so she could peek around the corner.

"Oh no you don't." She'd recognize Rex's smarmy voice any day. He circled his arms around her chest and yanked her backward. She stumbled a few steps, nearly toppling over.

"Drop your weapon," he growled.

Missy froze. "What's going on?"

"Nothing that concerns you, Sheriff. Just tying up loose ends. We've got places to be." Rex ran his fingers along Missy's arm, reaching for the gun she still had in her hand. "Give me your weapon." He moved his other arm and pressed his own gun to the side of Missy's head. "Or this will be the end of the road for you too."

"Okay, okay," Missy's mouth was dry and her adrenaline was pumping hard. She relaxed her arm, bringing the gun closer to Rex's reach.

Instead of fighting to get away from him, Missy leaned back and let her body drop like a sack of potatoes, taking him by surprise. She moved so fast that Rex didn't have time to react. She dropped, gun in hand, spun and hooked his knee with her arm, then rolled him down with her. It all happened in a matter of seconds. Rex hit the ground with a hard thud and a surprised grunt. Missy jumped to her feet then stomped on Rex's elbow until he released his gun. She kicked it away before taking aim with hers.

"Stay down!" she shouted. "Or this will be the end of the road for *you*."

Rex's eyes were wide as he raised his hands. "Now, now, Sheriff. There's no need to us to go down this path. We can work out a deal, I'm sure." He motioned behind him with his thumb. "I've got a car waiting. We can get out of here. I can set you up with a lot of money, give you a good life."

"I have a good life," she barked. "Now shut the fuck up! I'm not going anywhere with you." She readjusted her stance.

"Missy!"

She didn't look away from Rex, not for a second. She didn't have to. "I'm out here."

Adam came barreling out of the barn looking wild-eyed and ready to rip someone to pieces. His body was so pumped up that he seemed double his usual size. "Are you okay?" He took in the scene—Rex on the ground, his hands up, Missy pointing her gun at him, and Adam relaxed.

"I'm okay," she said. "I've got zip ties in my pocket." She nodded toward Rex.

Adam nodded then got to work incapacitating Rex.

"Rex Cooper, you're under arrest," Missy said.

"DEA, everyone put your weapons down!" a booming voice echoed from behind them.

She could see movement on the periphery.

Adam snapped his head around. Missy raised her hands, taking her finger off the trigger. "I'm Sheriff Alderton. My badge is in my pocket."

The DEA agent didn't hesitate. He reached into her pocket and pulled out her badge. "Okay, Sheriff, you're good. I'm Special Agent Danby."

Another agent came in behind Adam, a gun pointed at his head.

"This is my deputy, Adam Lancaster," Missy said as she lowered her arms and accepted her badge back.

Special Agent Danby motioned for the other agent to lower his weapon. "Adam Lancaster, deputy for Grimshield and bodyguard to Sabine Cowan?"

Adam nodded. "A man of many talents."

"So I've heard." Agent Danby nodded down at Rex. "This is the man we're here for, I presume?"

"Rex Cooper." Missy nodded. "Visiting scumbag."

The other agent got to work manhandling Rex to his feet. "We've got it from here, Sheriff. This is a federal matter now," Special Agent Danby said.

Missy nodded. "He's all yours."

"There are a couple of guys up the road," Adam said as he motioned behind him. "About a mile."

Danby nodded. "We'll get someone on that." He holstered his gun. "Read him his rights and get him in the truck." He turned back to Missy. "I'll have some questions for you later."

"My office is in Grimshield." She pulled a business card from her pocket and handed it to the agent. "I need to get back there and make sure everything is okay." She pointed to the barn. "You'll find my other deputy, Steve Webber, unconscious in there. He's part of this too. He was holding me hostage."

"Nephew to Commissioner Richardson," Danby said. "He's another one on our list. We've got the commissioner in custody already, along with his brother Neil." He tapped his earpiece, listening to someone on the other end. "We've got Tom Lancaster in custody. A relation of yours?"

"My brother," Adam said.

"He's a person of interest," Danby said. "You may want to call a lawyer on his behalf."

Missy winced. Hopefully Tommy would be a little bit more forthcoming with the DEA than he had been with her.

"Is he being arrested?" Adam asked.

"Held for questioning."

Missy had no doubt that Adam would take care of his brother in whatever way he could. No matter how many mistakes Tommy made, Adam cared enough to bail him out.

Adam nodded. "What happened with Sabine? Did she meet with Elton?"

Danby snapped his eyes over to Adam. "We've got him, too, thanks to Ms. Cowan." And by the way he pressed his lips together, Missy could tell that that was all he'd say about that.

Missy looked over at Adam and wondered just how connected his boss was. The woman was way more powerful than Missy had ever anticipated—and apparently on the side of the good guys after all.

"We've been investigating these men for some time. Couldn't nail them down until now. We'll take care of things from here, Sheriff. You can get back to taking care of your town."

"Thank you. I'll get my report together and share it with you asap." Missy sidestepped the agents and beelined for Adam. "Are you okay?" He didn't look like he was hurt, just scuffed up a bit.

"I'm good. You?" They were standing within in reach of one another but neither made a move to close the gap.

"I'm tired." And she was. Bone tired. All the adrenaline was out of her system and her legs felt wobbly. "I need to get back to the office and take care of the paperwork, make some calls."

"We'll get you back to Grimshield," Danby said.

"You need to go home and get some sleep. These guys have got everything under control. Your job is done for the day." Adam nodded. "Come on. You're dead on your feet."

Missy glanced over at the agents who were busy rounding up the rest of Rex's guys. The scumbags were officially leaving her jurisdiction. Grimshield was safe again. And now that she was down a man, she might actually have to put Adam to work as deputy until she could find a replacement. Then again, now that this was all over, he'd likely be heading home. She sighed inwardly. She was just too tired to think about this. Adam was right. She needed some sleep. "All right, Deputy Lancaster, take me home."

Adam laughed as he wrapped his arm around her shoulders. "Sure thing, boss." As soon as they cleared the side of the barn, he pulled her into his arms and kissed her so thoroughly that she actually thought there might be a future for them after all.

Chapter Twenty

Missy didn't want to wake up. On some level of consciousness, she knew she'd been sleeping for a long time, but on another level, she knew that the second she opened her eyes, she'd lose the delicious dream of Adam she was having.

"You're all tied up." Adam's husky voice cut through her brain, pulling her back into the fantasy she'd been enjoying.

She was tied up in the barn, her arms stretched above her head and her toes barely reaching the ground. There was no sign of Rex or the DEA agents. It was just her and Adam, all alone.

"Aren't you going to cut me down?" Her own voice sounded throaty and her body seemed to arch toward Adam like it had a mind of its own.

Adam's eyes flashed with mischief as he stalked closer, one hand rubbing his scruffy jaw, the other in his pocket. "Hmmm, maybe not."

She tugged at the rope that bound her wrists together. "Adam, someone could walk in!" And the thrill of that had her body revving all over again.

"I know," Adam said as he moved in close. "Don't you want someone to see us?"

He kissed along her collarbone, his body pressing into her slightly — just a tease, really. She shivered. "I-I-I don't know." He trailed his lips along her throat and his fingers played with the button of her uniform.

"I know." He popped the first button, then the next, all the while he sucked and licked his way over her skin.

Her nipples were tight, her pussy clenching. She knew she was so damn wet, and all she wanted was for him to slip his cock inside and pump her hard. He moved his other hand down to her belt and started the maddeningly slow process of unbuckling her.

"Adam," she moaned.

"Missy," he said back. But he didn't stop the slow progression of his lips and his hands. One more button of her shirt undone, then the next, until she felt the cool air hit her lace-covered tits.

She was burning up, hot as fuck, and she wanted Adam naked and inside her. "Take your clothes off," she whispered.

Adam stopped and looked up at her with that twinkle in his eyes again. Then he got out his phone and started scrolling.

What the...? "Adam, I said I want to see you naked!" She tugged on the rope. Her body was aching for this man and here he was checking his phone?

Music filled the barn. Loud, pumping, grinding kind of music. Missy flicked her eyes to the large barn doors. "Adam, someone will hear us."

He shrugged before putting the phone down on a nearby ledge. "Then they're in for a show."

That was when it clicked. That was when Adam started to dance.

He moved his body in a way that would seem impossible for such a huge guy – fluid, to the beat, like he'd taken dance lessons or something.

He stared straight into her eyes when he started to yank his shirt up, moving with the song to slowly reveal his abs and chest.

God, this man… He made her melt in all the right places.

He whipped his shirt off and tossed it her way before dancing some more. He looked like one of those professional exotic dancers and she was so happy that she had him all to herself.

He unbuttoned his pants next and her breath caught. She loved his dick. It was not only huge, but it was thick and curved a bit so that when he wedged himself deep inside her, he hit every single erogenous zone she had down there.

He let his pants drop. His cock was hard, impressive as usual, and on display. Thank fuck this man didn't prefer underwear.

She rocked her hips, wishing she were naked too, no longer caring that anyone could walk in and see them. She wanted him to nail her to the post with his dick.

The music died and Adam stopped dancing. "I want you, Missy. Always have, always will."

She whimpered. "I want you too."

He was on her in a flash. Ripping her clothes from her body like they were made of tissue paper. It all happened so quickly that Missy didn't have to wait for long to feel the press of his body against hers. His delicious scent invaded her nose in an instant and she lifted her legs to wrap around his waist so he could slip that juicy cock of his deep inside.

With one hand playing with her tit and the other holding her up, his cock pressed just at her entrance, he paused again so he could look into her eyes. "Missy, I want a life with you."

She gasped, but he held her stare like he was serious.

"I-I-I d-d-o too," she said.

He leaned down and kissed her. Tongue tangled with tongue, lips on lips, it was a kiss to beat all kisses because with it came the thrust of his massive cock into her soaking wet pussy.

The cascading rush of her mounting climax had her gasping through their kiss. Had she ever felt something so wonderful? Only with Adam.

Missy woke with a start, the remnants of her orgasm still causing her pussy to spasm. *Well, that's something new.* She'd never come in a dream before. With Adam around, though, it seemed anything was possible.

It took her body a bit to relax and her brain to stop stumbling over the idea of Adam fucking her brains out back at that barn. What a strange fantasy to have. And yet, with Adam, not strange at all.

The words he'd said to her in her dream had felt so real. Figments of her imagination, wishful thoughts, of course, but all the same, she felt them deep in her soul.

She scanned her bedroom. Adam wasn't there. She felt the instant weight of disappointment. Had he left while she had been sleeping? Was he back on a plane to New York? Missy checked the time. It was night. She'd slept the day away. There had been plenty of time for him to get back to his life in the city, especially if he caught a ride back home with his boss on her private jet.

Missy rubbed her hand over her face and sighed. If she were going to be honest, she was more than disappointed. She was crushed. He'd said he'd wanted to see where things would go with them. Maybe he meant the next time he decided to fly back to Grimshield.

But no, that wasn't the way it had seemed when they had been talking. *Ugh.* Her self-doubt was getting the better of her.

She remembered Adam bringing her home, her taking her clothes off and crawling into bed. She even remembered Adam climbing in with her and wrapping her up in his arms, whispering things to her that made her feel good…loved…but words that she just couldn't grasp onto now. Did he say he was leaving? Did he wait until she was just asleep before slipping out? She'd been so damn tired that she just couldn't remember anything but drifting off to sleep.

She sighed again. Could she blame him if he left? Things were settled here and his family was safe. Missy would be able to get the town back to normal with Rex and his thugs out of the way. And frankly, the town was usually very quiet under normal circumstances. Adam likely had things to do for his boss.

But still… She kinda wanted a bit more time with Adam right now.

She found her phone charging on her night table. There were missed calls from some of her law enforcement contacts. The deputy commissioner had reached out to her. He wasn't a bad guy—fair, reasonable—and also, if she remembered correctly, not a huge fan of the amalgamation idea that Richardson had begun to put into place the past year. Maybe Missy could convince the acting commissioner to throw her a bit of money so she could hire some more staff.

Her phone dinged with a few incoming texts, none from Adam. Lacey wanted to know if she was okay. A few other townspeople were asking for updates now that Rex was gone.

Shit. She'd slept long enough. Time to shower and get to work. She'd deal with the Adam situation and her feelings about that later.

She walked naked down to the washroom — There was no point in throwing on clothes when she was just going to take them off again. Besides, she lived alone anyway, so there was no one to see her strutting down the hall. She scanned the living room just before she stepped into the bathroom, hoping that maybe, just maybe, there'd be a sign of Adam. *Nope.* The room was empty.

Adam was gone.

Her heart did that weird 'I'm going to die' twist that had her lifting her knuckles to rub her chest.

Get a grip!

She'd survived him leaving before. She'd do it again.

But still…it hurt. Not even a text? He could have at least left a note or something.

With a shake of her head and tears burning the back of her eyes, she stepped into the washroom. *Time to get on with the day.*

She showered quickly and got the grit and grime out of her hair from the barn experience and rolling around in the dirt with Rex. She was just getting out and wrapping a towel around her body when she heard someone coming through the front door.

Ah shit! Her gun was in the bedroom.

With her hair dripping over her shoulders, she quietly opened the door and peered down the hall. She could make it to her room in three seconds.

She didn't even have time to step one foot out of the bathroom when Adam came strolling around the corner. He pulled up short when he saw her, his eyes going wide. "Well now, Missy, you couldn't wait for me before you got all soapy?"

Um... Her mouth went completely dry. Adam was there and he was wearing a— "Where did you get a uniform?" He was dressed like a proper deputy should be, minus the utility belt with a gun holster. Instead, he had his own belt around his waist, the one he always seemed to be wearing.

"I have my ways." He winked then gave her a steamy full-body sweep.

"And you went out and about dressed like that?" The town folk would be so confused.

"Well, I am still your deputy, aren't I?" He motioned to the badge on his chest. "I found this in your desk."

"You were snooping in my desk?" Missy couldn't keep the smile off her face despite the fact that she felt so foolish for thinking he'd left. "That's not in your job description!"

"I wasn't snooping. I was investigating. I swept your office, found the bugs Steve planted, documented everything, collected evidence bags, the whole nine yards. DEA will pick it up tomorrow. Thought I'd be useful since you were out cold." The smile he flashed back at her made her heart soar. "Once I was done with that, I thought I'd get the lay of the land, introduce myself to people who may not know me, sort out some business."

"You've been working?"

Adam shrugged. "I left you a note on the fridge."

"And what about your job in New York?" Missy couldn't believe her ears.

"I told Sabine that I'll be working remotely for a while." His smile went all crooked. "I figured it would give you time to find a proper deputy and give us time to figure out what we want from each other."

She wasn't delusional. She knew he wouldn't be able to stay in Grimshield forever, but she hadn't expecting this either. Crap, a bit ago she'd been convinced that he'd left without saying goodbye. "Makes sense." And it did. She wanted the time to explore things with Adam, to see how they could make things more permanent if they wanted to. She was playing it cool, but really, her heart was doing flip-flops.

"Besides, my mom really loved seeing me in this uniform." He brushed his hand down his chest.

Missy also really loved seeing him in that uniform. She nodded. "It looks good on you."

He quirked a sly smile. "So, are we having a shower now or what?"

"I just had a shower." But she'd do it again if it included Adam.

He moved toward her, his eyes all hooded and sexy. "I think you need another one."

He started unbuttoning his shirt and, holy shit, it was an instant flashback to her dream. "Actually." She held up her hand and moved towards him. "I'm kind of thinking I'd like to see you take that uniform off in my bedroom." She let the towel drop and moved in so close that her nipples rubbed against the fabric of his shirt. She went up on tiptoes. "I want to see you strip."

He looked down at her, his eyes dark, blasting her with all his sexy hotness, but didn't make any moves to touch her. "How'd you know that was my specialty?"

She laughed. "I had a dream about it."

Chapter Twenty-One

He followed her sexy, heart-shaped ass all the way to the bedroom. "Hop up on the bed, sweetheart, and let me give you a show."

Missy gave him a raised-eyebrow look as she glanced at him over her shoulder while at the same time slowly climbing onto the bed on all fours.

Fuck, she was so damn hot. Everything about her made his body jolt with arousal, even more so because she didn't know how hot she was.

She moved slowly up to the head of the bed. Adam got to work removing his belt. It was a delicate procedure because he didn't want the blades to flip out by accident and damage the belt loops on his new pants.

"Wait just one minute!" Missy had her hand up and her eyes glued to his waist. "Show me that belt."

Adam grinned as he slowly finished taking the belt off. He moved to the side of the bed, his belt stretched out across his palms.

Missy looked from the belt to him, her eyes wide. "This is how you did it, isn't it?" She ran a finger along the length of it.

"Watch yourself," Adam warned, then he pulled back a bit and clicked the blades up. There were four, only about an inch and a half in length, but they were all wicked sharp.

Missy gasped. "I'll be damned! I knew you couldn't bust out of those zip ties with just brute strength."

Adam laughed. "Are you saying I'm not strong enough?"

Missy cocked an eyebrow as she looked up at him. "I'm saying that as impressive as you are, there's no way you could get out of police-grade plastic ties. But if you'd like to prove me wrong, we could give it a go right now—after you're naked."

Adam shook his head and slowly walked backward until he got to the end of the bed. "Turn the music on, smartass."

She laughed but did as she was told. Within seconds the sound of a good bass-thumping tune blasted from her phone and Adam got down to business.

After working security for Sabine for so many years and having spent a lot of that time in many of her Kitty Cat clubs, Adam knew a thing or two about stripping.

He knew how to move his body to get the best reaction, and while the space wasn't big enough for him to do any flips or splits, he could put on a good show for Missy. He started with his shirt, moving his body at the same time as he unbuttoned. He worked quickly so that he could open his shirt to reveal his chest and abs, then he flexed, making sure that the cut of his muscles was exaggerated. He turned so his back was toward her then pulled his shirt down to mid-back.

He flexed again, glancing over his shoulder at her at the same time. Missy licked her lips. Her eyes were riveted to his body and he liked that. He turned again and began to slip his shirt off his arms.

And froze.

Missy was snaking her hand down her glorious body. Right down the center, between her perfect tits, straight to her— "Don't stop, Adam."

He snapped himself out of his momentary stupor then flung his shirt off. He needed to speed this along, because Missy's fingers were sliding between her pussy lips and his cock was aching to do the same.

He unbuttoned his pants and teased with the zipper.

Missy's eyes went wide. "Don't stop." She spread her legs and slid her fingers right inside her slick-looking hole.

Mmm-m, fuck, yeah. Adam let his pants drop. His cock was jutting out painfully. He held it in his hand and began to stroke just as Missy did the same against her clit.

"Striptease is over," he announced as he climbed up onto the bed, jostling her in his haste.

She let out a husky, sexy laugh followed by a deep moan once he supplemented her finger action with his tongue and lips. God, she tasted so good. He lapped her up, rolling his tongue over and over until her body was writhing. She moved both of her hands to her tits and was flicking and rubbing her hard, little nipples. Her eyes were on him, watching as he licked and sucked.

"I want to taste you too," she moaned.

Of course, that was the best idea ever. It took some positioning—sometimes being a big guy got in the way of the simple things—but Adam moved so that his cock was positioned right at her lips. She didn't keep him waiting. He slipped his fingers into her pussy just as she latched on to his cock with her warm, wet mouth. The dual sensation of licking and stroking Missy at the same time as she did it to him was better than any drug he'd ever had in his life. It was all-consuming, rolling waves of pleasure, an ever-building orgasm that Adam thought would never crest.

If only he could let his rising orgasm go on forever — longer than forever. It just felt so damn good.

And when it did crest, holy fuck. It was like an explosion and he saw stars. He pumped Missy full of his cum and she swallowed it down. She arched her lower body into his mouth at the same time, her pussy contracting so intensely that she was squeezing his fingers.

Once they were spent, he rolled to the side. Missy flipped around so that they could lie face-to-face. She was flushed with color and breathing hard.

"It's always so amazing with you." She reached up to touch his jaw.

"I knew it would be from the moment I first saw you."

Missy made a face. "You first saw me when I was, like, five."

He shook his head and pulled her into his arms. "No, I mean, from the moment I first *really* saw you."

"At the Halloween party," she said with a quick of a smile.

"I knew that you were the perfect kind of girl for me right in that moment."

"Because I was dressed up like a sexy angel and was ready to fuck your brains out?"

"No, because only a brave, bold, in-charge kind of woman would have the nerve to do what you did that night. That's the right kind of woman for me."

Missy smiled. "I always knew you were the right kind of guy for me. Something drew me to you right from the time that I was a kid, and it has never gone away."

Adam moved closer so he could touch his lips to hers gently, tenderly. "I'll stay here as long as you need me to."

"You can't stay here forever, Adam." She cleared her throat and pulled back a bit. Her smile was gone. "Sabine needs you."

"I've devoted myself to Sabine for a long time, and I appreciate all of the opportunities she's given me. But work is work. It isn't all there is to life. And when you find someone..." He paused and smiled. "I mean, *see* someone again, who you truly love, someone you've wanted to be with for a very long time, then you need to reset priorities. Sabine understands that."

Missy gulped. He could practically see her mind working.

"I bet I could talk the deputy commissioner into hiring more deputies so that I can take the vacation time I never seem to be able to get." Her lips curled into a smile. "I've always wondered about New York, what it's like."

"Have you?" Adam couldn't keep the smile from his face. He was willing to sacrifice a lot to keep Missy in his life, but Sabine had already told him that if he split his time between Montana and New York, she'd be okay with that. She'd miss him, sure, but a lot of his job could be done remotely, and he'd trained his crew to be stellar bodyguards. Sabine was covered and she wanted Adam to be happy. "I could take you to a few places I'll bet you've never been to before."

Missy laughed. "I bet you could." She kissed him then, deeply, her tongue stroking his with so much passion, so much emotion, that Adam could feel it in every move she made.

He rolled her under his body, taking care not to put his full weight on her, and nudged himself between her legs. "I'm not sheathed," he said as he stared down at her. "But I've been tested. I'm clean."

Missy nodded. "I'm clean too and I trust you."

She wrapped her legs around his waist as best she could and urged him to push inside. Skin-on-skin was something he hadn't ever experienced in his life. He'd been waiting for the right opportunity and the right person. He knew, without a doubt, that Missy was the one.

He slid his dick home and shuddered with pleasure when he felt the soft, wet cushion of her pussy taking him in, accommodating his girth and holding on. They fit together perfectly, their bodies as one. As he rocked his hips, held her close and she arched up, their eyes were locked, and for the first time, they made love.

"You're my woman now."

"And you're my man," Missy agreed. She lifted her hands and ran them through his hair then brought his head down so she could kiss him again.

Tongues entangled, bodies entwined, they stroked each other in every right way. Their orgasms came in unison, a slow roll of pleasure that Adam felt along every nerve ending, jolting him until he was spewing cum deep into Missy and her pussy gripped him with waves of intensity until they were both completely spent.

E p i l o g u e

Six months later

Missy had never been to New York before and this trip was turning out to be filled with a lot of firsts. It was her first time flying on a private jet, her first time seeing the Statue of Liberty in person and her first time going to a Kitty Cat Club and seeing a whole lotta sexy girls taking their clothes off.

She'd never realized how erotic it actually was to witness a professional doing her thing. The Kitty Cats were all sexy, sultry women, all with different body types, all moving to the beat of the music in a way that showcased their assets. The club itself was low-key, with private booths that kept each patron from seeing the next. Missy was sitting next to Adam, her fingers entwined with his, her eyes wide.

This is amazing!

She had no idea what she'd been missing out on.

"They are so beautiful." She had to shout to be heard above the thumping music.

Adam squeezed her hand and nodded. She knew he was watching her, gauging her reaction. In the six months that they'd been officially together, Missy had learned a lot about Adam's life in New York and also about Sabine's various businesses. She'd heard about the different ways that Sabine took care of the women working for her. She'd come to understand how empowered these women actually were. They did hold the power, *always*.

Adam had told her so many stories about the Kitty Cats and his interactions with them too, that she was definitely intrigued and, strangely, not at all jealous. When Missy had finally gotten the opportunity to use her accumulated vacation time, she'd known she needed to see some of this for herself.

The girls on the stage were using the poles in ways that Missy had never thought possible. They could lift themselves in incredible, gravity-defying holds just with the sheer power of their arms and abs. They knew just how to display their gorgeous bodies with so much power and grace that Missy found herself wondering if she could learn how to do the flips and twists. It was sensual and Missy's whole body was on fire. She looked at Adam, locking eyes with him. He had that glint, the unmistakable dare that seemed to always be present. How far would she go with this man? The limit to how far she would go was yet to be determined.

She wanted him now, like every moment of every day.

Her cheeks heated, but all the same, she looked around, judging if anyone would see them.

He squeezed her hand. "No one will notice," he said, his lips so close to her ear that she could hear him perfectly. "No one will care."

He'd already assured her that the media couldn't get close to the club they were in and cell phones were collected at the door. She felt safe and yet, she wanted to be naughty too.

He nudged her, indicating that she should shift onto his lap.

She looked at him again. He was grinning.

It wasn't like they hadn't done this before.

It wasn't like she hadn't fantasized about fucking him in public again.

She shifted onto his lap, so that she was facing the dancers. His cock was hard and pressing into her back.

He slipped his hands to her thighs and started to push her skirt up. She shivered. Were they really going to do this? It seemed like anything was possible when Adam was around, not that she minded. Being with Adam was the only thing she wanted. Her lust for him and her love for him were all-consuming.

She watched the dancers as they took their clothes off and moved their bodies. It was so hot, so incredibly sexy. Missy ran her hands over her breasts, just like one of the girls did. Her nipples budded into hard nubs under her clothes. It was maddening that she couldn't take her clothes off too. Maybe she'd be able to use some of the moves she was seeing now later at Adam's condo.

She pushed herself back so she could rub Adam's dick with her ass. His hands were still working her skirt up. She felt the cool air hit her bare pussy. She'd stopped wearing panties, thanks to Adam. It was one less barrier when they wanted to fuck.

The touch of his fingers against her clit made her jolt then moan, because he didn't waste any time. He slipped his fingers inside her, using his palm to rub her roughly. She pushed against him, grinding his cock with her ass until she could feel that he was so fucking hard she knew he wouldn't be able to take it much longer.

He loved public displays of affection, something she'd gotten used to. But this? This was fantasy material. Missy's imagination knew no bounds.

She eased herself forward, then reached behind her and popped the button on his pants. She tugged down his zipper and his cock sprang right out. He leaned into her, nipped her ear then growled.

"Just like old times," he said, sending a shiver down her spine.

She eased herself back and he slipped his fingers out of her pussy and replaced them with his cock.

It was exhilarating! And yes, just like their first time. Missy was bombarded by sensations, pure pleasure, excitement and the feeling of being extremely naughty. Every fantasy she'd ever had, Adam fulfilled. Every sexual desire she'd ever wanted, Adam gave to her. Even things she didn't know she wanted—he made sure they happened. Like watching sexy women strip for her and her boyfriend… Now she knew how erotic it was and she wanted more.

With Adam, everything and more was possible.

She moved slowly, riding him with a deliberate grind, leaning back so that he braced her against his hard chest and caged her breasts with his massive arm. His other hand moved to her pussy, rubbing her clit with his expert fingers. She felt protected. She felt cherished.

As her climax began to rise and her body responded to Adam's in the most familiar way, Missy couldn't help but feel the all-consuming rush of being truly in love with someone and knowing that Adam felt the same way about her.

What adventures lie before us?

Considering how this relationship had started, with a naughty-angel costume a dare from a friend...well, Missy believed the possibilities were endless.

Want to see more from this author?
Here's a taster for you to enjoy!

Naughty or Nice?:
Wicked Christmas
Angela Addams

Excerpt

Vivian Hayes lived for the holiday season. She adored all the fuss of decorating trees and putting up lights. She looked forward to the festivities and the cheer. She enjoyed wrapping up presents and she absolutely *loved* receiving them.

"Hmm-m, what do we have here?" She ran her freshly manicured nails—she'd gone with silver sparkles—along the length of Lucas' rock-hard cock. "An early Christmas present?" He was wearing a Santa hat and nothing else, which was a glorious sight to see. He had an athletic build because he was a swimmer, lean and powerful. His ab muscles were taut, ready for her tongue to trace along each valley on her way down to his long, thick cock. The fact that he'd waltzed into her home office naked but for his hat told her she'd worked way past her usual quitting time.

"We thought you should know that we ordered take-out," Lucas said with a grin. "But it won't be here for forty-five minutes."

"So we have time to blow off a little steam," James said as he walked into her office with one of his signature martinis in hand and a pair of nipple clamps dangling off his finger. He was completely naked too — well, except for one part of him.

Vivian let out of short laugh. "Is that a Christmas stocking on your dick?"

James stopped so he could showcase his package. "You want to peek inside?" He rolled his hips before thrusting out his cock.

"Wouldn't that put me on the naughty list?" Vivian purred as she stood from her chair and moved around her desk. Lucas started to unbutton her blouse, his eyes hooded and full of lust.

"Aren't you *always* on the naughty list?" James stepped closer so he could hand her the martini. "Sour Apple with a twist of caramel."

"Mmm-m, you do spoil me." Vivian took a deep drink and closed her eyes as the tart flavor exploded on her tongue first, followed by the sweet caramel chaser. "This is delicious."

Lucas helped her out of her blouse then unhooked her bra so she could take that off too. He was always so gentle with her to start, knowing what she needed before even she knew. She turned her head so she could kiss him. His lips tasted like cinnamon and were soft yet firm. He stroked her mouth lazily with his tongue, taking his time as he ran his fingers along the plane of her stomach.

James took the martini out of her hand, but she didn't get a chance to protest because he clamped her nipples. She moaned into Lucas' mouth from both the exquisite pleasure and the sharp pain.

"You've been working so hard," James said. "Vacation starts *now*."

She broke off the kiss with Lucas. He continued working on her clothes, shifting down her body so he could undo her skirt. James moved in, running his hand up her spine until he gripped the back of her neck. His eyes were full of mischief and, like his brother, full on pussy-weeping desire. *Fuck, these boys are so hot, and they know exactly how to make me wet.*

Vivian smiled up at James just as Lucas dropped her skirt to her ankles. "Well, I needed to wrap some things up before we head to Mom's tomorrow." She was taking Lucas and James home to meet her mom and stepdad for the first time. "Sabine wanted a few cost projections for two of the Kitty Cat parties coming up."

A former Kitty Cat herself, Vivian understood exactly what needed to get done to satisfy her boss, Sabine Cowan. It was nothing short of perfection, and Vivian was the girl for the job. She was always super-organized and knew how to negotiate the right price for the merch she needed. Sabine had seen her potential right from the get-go and had started her party planning almost from the beginning. Now she was the head buyer for all the Kitty Cat Boutiques and Salons, as well as for the fetish and lingerie lines — something she was very proud of.

"I trust you got everything done that needed to be completed?" James asked before drinking down the rest of her martini.

Vivian shrugged one shoulder. "Of course." Then she let him take her mouth, his forceful kiss letting her know just what the next forty-five minutes would entail.

He would know that she needed to get some energy out after spending all day on the computer and phone. He brushed the nipple clamps with the edge of his martini glass. It clanked against the metal and made Vivian hiss from the jarring pain and the slow burn that came after.

Lucas had her skirt and panties off and, between the two of them, they eased her back onto her desk, clearing away the clutter so that she was comfortable. Lucas splayed her aching pussy with his deft fingers and got to work on her clit—sucking, nipping and overall giving her exactly what she needed right fucking *now*.

James moved to her head on the other side of the desk and offered up his dick. "Peel the stocking off, baby. I know you want to."

With a wicked grin, she ran her nails up his cock to where the stocking met his skin. It was red-and-white knitted, with little puffy balls of gold decorating the length, and it fit his dick perfectly. She wanted to know where he'd found it, partly because she thought it would be a big seller at some of the boutiques and also because she wanted one on Lucas as well. She cupped his balls and slowly began to peel the stocking off. "What a lovely surprise." As usual, his huge cock was hard as hell. "I'd like to give it a taste."

James grinned. "By all means." She pulled the stocking off completely and turned her head farther to the side so she could guide his dick straight into her mouth.

"Mmm-m," she moaned as his cock stretched out her lips almost to the point of pain.

He eased himself in, all the way to the back of her throat. The taste his pre-cum coating her tongue with its salty tang made her pussy weep even more. She tightened her lips and hummed, letting the vibration tickle his flesh, then reached up with one hand to cup his balls again. James' eyes were hooded and his body swayed closer. He put his hand over her breast, jolting her as he pressed against one of the nipple clamps. Her body pulsed with arousal, her nerve endings pinging with pain and pleasure all mixed. Lucas was using his tongue against her clit, alternating between flicking lightly and applying pressure as needed, and his fingers were wedged deep inside, stroking her G-spot. Viv was sure she hadn't felt so damn good all day.

* * * *

By the time the food arrived, they were sweaty and ravenous. They sat on the floor, cushioned by oversized pillows, around the coffee table. The TV was muted, but there was a classic Christmas movie playing, and Vivian couldn't help but feel like this was the last time for the next seven days that she'd have her boys to herself.

"Mom is really excited to meet you two," she said between forkfuls of fried rice.

Vivian's mom was totally cool with her dating two men, two *brothers*, but all the same, Vivian was feeling a little anxious about the home visit.

"She bought you matching Christmas ugly sweaters. I tried to tell her that you aren't identical twins but she was adamant that you needed to both be wearing the same thing for the family photo."

Lucas gave her his last spring roll, likely because he knew they were her favorite, and he also knew that if he didn't act fast, James would steal it right off his plate. "We haven't had a real family Christmas in a very long time." He reminded her with a kiss on the cheek. "We'll happily do whatever your mom wants us to do."

"Well, except for singing carols," James grimaced. "You don't want to hear us try to do that, especially with this guy's booming vocals." He pointed his thumb at his brother, who threw a pillow at him in return.

"At least I know better than to even try to sing. I hear you in the shower, James, and you sound like a screeching cat."

Vivian smiled. *Fuck, I love these guys.* "I can't believe you're willing to spend the next seven days in snowy Pennsylvania, when you could be catching rays on some tropical beach somewhere." Which was what Vivian had done the previous year with a bunch of the Kitty Cats, since it hadn't been her year to spend back home.

James pulled her onto his lap so quickly that she almost dropped her drink. "Oh, baby, all we want for Christmas is you," he sang, off key and croaky. Before she could laugh, he was punishing her with another one of his brutal kisses, letting her know how much he wanted her.

"We love the snow!" Lucas said once James put her back on her pillow. He flashed her a toothy grin and added, "We want to spend Christmas with you and your family. There's no other place in the world we'd rather be. Right, James?"

"Hell yes!" James swiped the spring roll off Vivian's plate and bit it in half. "I want to ravage you under the mistletoe."

"Hey! I wanted that!" She swatted his hand. He had the sense to look guilty when he offered the last bite of her spring roll to her. "Sorry. I'm just *so* hungry!"

"You're always hungry," Vivian laughed. And he was — always hungry for her, for food, for chocolate, for ice cream. The man could eat like nothing she'd ever seen before. Her mom would love that about him. "Go ahead and eat it. I've had enough." Her phone dinged and she checked the text. "Oh good, the dildos have arrived at Mom's."

"Now that's something you don't hear every day." James snorted.

"For the sex-toy party?" She rolled her eyes. Her mom had asked her to set something up, a fun, sexy little party for her book club friends who had all recently discovered erotic romance. Vivian's mom was never one to shy away from trying something new and she had insisted that Vivian bring all the good gear—kinky stuff too—so that she and her friends could see what was out there.

"I told you, James." Lucas started packing up the food. "We're going to be display models that day, showing off the products for the ladies."

"So I should pack my thongs? Maybe the red-and-green ones, you know, so I'll be festive?"

Vivian's memory flashed to James wearing a thong and how his tight ass looked in them. "Oh yeah, you definitely should." She nodded, her face heating at the idea of her boyfriend flashing all his goodies for her mother's friends. "The ladies will love that, and Mom will make more money for her charity endeavor."

Her mom was trying to save a building, an old barn that was home to a colony of feral cats. The barn and its accompanying farmhouse had been built in 1892 and was the responsibility of the town to maintain. But like all century-old buildings, it was a money pit. The house was in near-ruins but the barn was in relatively good shape, thanks in part to Vivian's mom and her friends and all their charity runs. Her mom had come up with the idea of the sex-toy party when Vivian had confirmed she'd be able to make it home for the holidays.

"And definitely the Santa hat," Lucas said as he leaned into her, wrapping his arm around her waist and pulling her closer.

She draped her arms over his shoulders and laughed as he heaved her up, cradling her in his arms. "And the cock stocking should get packed too." She looked over at James, who was stalking toward them on all fours, looking all predatory and ready to eat her up. He had a pair of loose track pants on, but she could see his cock jutting already. "I think the ladies will love that the best."

"That is for your eyes only, baby," James growled. He leaned in and nuzzled her neck, nipping her earlobe before pulling away. "I think you're going to need a little punishing before we leave."

Vivian's nodded eagerly. Her body was on fire already, her pussy aching for James' kind of punishment. Lucas lifted her as he stood, an impressive display of his strength, then turned on his heel and started for the bedroom. "Maybe we should get the paddles out."

Vivian knew she wouldn't be getting very much sleep before their flight the next morning, with the mood the boys were in — not that she was complaining. She'd take everything they had to give and more. Besides, that was what she'd signed up for when she'd agreed to date them both.

Really, with such gorgeous men willing to make her happy, why have one boyfriend when she could have two?

Home of Erotic Romance

Sign up for our newsletter and find out about all our romance book releases, eBook sales and promotions, sneak peeks and FREE romance books!

About the Author

Angela Addams is an author of many naughty things. She believes that the written word is an amazing tool for crafting the most erotic of scenarios and likes telling stories about normal people getting down and dirty and falling in love. Enthralled by the paranormal at an early age, Angela also spends a lot of her time thinking up new story ideas that involve supernatural creatures in everyday situations.

She is an avid tattoo collector, a total book hoarder, and loves anything covered in chocolate…except for bugs. She lives in Ontario, Canada in an old, creaky house, with her husband, children and four moody cats.

Angela loves to hear from readers. You can find her contact information, website details and author profile page at https://www.totallybound.com